GOING MY WAY

Tanja Tuma

Copyright © Tanja Tuma
www.tanjatuma.com
US Coryright Office #TXu 2-197-752
Copyedited by Arlene Ang
Cover design by Tadej Tuma

All events and characters in this book are fictitious.

All rights reserved. No part of this publication may be reproduced, stored in a retrieval system or transmitted in any form or by any means without the prior permission in writing of the publisher, nor be circulated in writing of any publisher, nor be otherwise circulated in any form of binding or cover other than that in which it is published without a similar condition including this condition, being imposed on the subsequent purchaser.

Self-Published in August 2020
ISBN: 979-8675251988

Prologue

> To see a World in a Grain of Sand
> And a Heaven in a Wild Flower,
> Hold Infinity in the palm of your hand
> And Eternity in an hour.
> A Robin Red breast in a Cage
> Puts all Heaven in a Rage.
>
> – William Blake, Auguries of Innocence

Death crawled on the linoleum floor, his sinister call echoing from the walls, his shadow on everybody's faces – doctors, nurses, patients, visitors. The silent certainty of human transience. The whitewashed corridors of the central university hospital were a one-way road to eternity.

Vera Lucca shivered with angst as she pushed the door handle. How was Adam doing? The horror of her husband's lifeless body on the floor was omnipresent. Last night he said he had things to do in the study, so she went to bed alone. She was used to it. In three decades of marriage, their love life took a slower pace. Gone was the passion of the old days when they could hardly wait for children to fall asleep, so they could light the fires of their loins in the secrecy of the bedroom. These days, their kids were living away from home. Their daughter Sarah got married and moved to Maribor, an industrial town in the East, still struggling with the economic crisis, the rustbelt of Slovenia. She had her own mind and never cared for her parents' advice. She was expecting her first child in the middle of her business studies. Their son Gregory was single, for his girlfriend had refused to follow him to South America. He was doing his PhD in biology, studying ants in Argentina.

Did Vera miss them? Not usually. She did not bring her children into this world with the intent of owning their lives forever. She was happy to set them free. As a rule. However, lately, she was concerned about her marriage. Adam had changed. He'd become moody and lost his temper quickly. She was trying to understand the reason behind this. Thoughts of a younger lover or troubles at work occurred to her. However, both seemed absurd.

Adam's business was thriving, and the women around him knew to keep their distance after all these years. Adam loved only her. He had shown Vera only endless affection and respect.

So, what was it?

What ghost had shattered their existence all of a sudden?

"Hello, darling. How are you feeling?" She approached his bed.

There was no sign of life on his face. A powerful sensation of loss overcame her. To her unease, she realized she was at the center of everyone's attention, all eyes in the room on her. The patients were males of different ages. Two around Adam's age, one old enough to be his father and two young men, nearly boys. One of the boys on the bed next to Adam seemed barely alive, all skin and bones. The visitors, sitting and standing around the other beds, were whispering softly. The air smelled badly of urine and disinfectant. The bed lamps emitted only a dim glow in the aisle between the beds. Autumn was coming, taking the light of day away before the sun could penetrate the frosted glass of the windows. Overwhelmed by emotion, she couldn't stop tears from running down her cheeks. Grey sorrow invaded her mind.

Adam had aged ten years since last night. Asleep, he could not hear Vera. His ashen face bespoke of pain she could not comprehend. Around her, the eyes of strangers filled with regret. Automatically, she grabbed the patient's chart pinned to Adam's bed.

"Pancreas adenocarcinoma."

What? They must be wrong. Adam could not have this. He was fit and always active. Just a week ago, they had gone on a trip to the seaside. They walked along the beaches, talked about old times, and had fish and scallops for dinner at a family restaurant with a view of Trieste where Adam grew up.

She was trying to understand the Latin abbreviations when Adam opened his eyes.

"It's okay, Vera. I feel better today," he said in a determined voice meaning "Put down that sheet." Should she tell him she had seen the diagnosis?

"Hi, darling." Vera hung the sheet back on the bed railing, kissed him on the cheeks and sat on his bed.

He watched her for a while, the air around them frozen into serene stillness.

"I...how can I tell you this?"

She caressed his palm gently. "Just tell me, Adam. It'll be fine."

He inhaled deeply. "I'm afraid it won't. Did you see what I have?"

Vera nodded, unable to speak, swallowing a sour lump in her throat.

"It is incurable. I don't have much time left."

Her face sank. "How long have you known?"

He looked out the window although the only view it offered was frosted glass. Never had he felt so alone. All those months of knowing, hiding. Why didn't he confide in her, his loving wife?

Down on the road, outside the hospital, they could hear the beeping and screeching of cars. Life continued its course in the streets below.

"For some time now," he finally said and looked her in the eye.

Oh, she could read his thoughts like an open book. He wanted to spare her the pain for as long as possible. Proud and noble, Adam could not stand pity. He was five years old the last time he'd found himself helpless and at mercy of the strangers. He had lost Mother. More correctly, she'd lost him on purpose. Adam was an orphan with scattered memories of where he came from. No family, no roots. Still, he went to school, excelling in business studies, and had built himself a family and a life. He had bootstrapped his insurance and finance company from zero. Now, it was one of the best in the region, expanding from Slovenia into Austria, Italy, and Croatia. Solid, prosperous, transparent. No monkey business, no foggy assets, no ill-gotten gains by privatization.

Until recently, the mechanism of Adam's life ticked like a perfect Swiss watch. It was after his regular medical checkup that he discovered the cause for the pain under his ribs and the stomach cramps he'd been ignoring for some time. His life collapsed like a house of cards. It was while thinking of how to regain control over his fate that he fainted in his study.

He had hesitated too long to tell Vera. She had to see the medical sheet. Was love his lame excuse for keeping his terminal disease from his family? As long as the cancer only dwelled within the whitewashed walls of the hospital, he could pretend he had a life ahead of him. Now, he could not. Game over, Adam.

Still, a pang of pain shook her. She was not a stranger. She was his wife for more than two decades. They had gone through difficult times and had faced death and its horrible schemes before.

"You know how much I love you, don't you, Vera?"

"I know, darling."

"Can you forgive me?"

Leaning forward, she laid her head on his chest. There it was; the beat of his heart. He held her in his arms, his right awkwardly entangled in the IV line. Vera was crying, her tears soaking the bed linen.

"I'm sorry, Adam. It is such a shock," she moaned between

sobs.

He caressed her back, trying to control his emotions. He didn't want to show distress in front of all these strangers.

Why aren't there privacy curtains or screens?

Why was his illness on display for everybody who happened to open the door?

"It's all right, darling. I should have told you earlier. I'm sorry," he said, his voice cracking.

For a moment, their roles reversed. He was trying to alleviate her pain, although his own pain would soon kill him. There was little chance to cure or control the growth of pancreatic cancer. How could this happen to him? Why him? This was evil. And he thought he had left evil behind. Yet, it had returned with its two faces, one looking back and the other forward, like the god Janus.

"We'll manage, Vera," he said, trying to stop her outburst. "We always have, darling."

Understanding his intention, she dried her tears with some paper towels from the bed stand.

"We must tell the kids," she said once she regained some control over her voice.

He shook his head in despair. "Not just yet, please. Let's first deal with the situation alone."

After a moment of silence, Vera replied, "I think you should tell them. You cannot exclude the children from your life because you're ill. It's not your fault, Adam. They'll understand."

Adam's voice trembled. "Vera, it is my life and my cancer – it will be my death. Please, let me find a way to deal with my life and my death as I wish."

His words hit her like a hammer striking a nail. He was too sick to bother with niceties.

"Can I ask for a favor?"

"Anything, Adam," she replied gloomily.

While focusing on his question, he stroked her hand. "The chief of gastroenterology, Dr. Janek, is receiving patients' relatives from one to two o'clock. Can you go and see him today,

Vera?"

She nodded, practical again. "Of course. You want me to ask about your condition, don't you?"

"Yeah, you know how doctors are. They think they should spare their patients the truth. Sometimes they don't tell us everything. But he'll tell you." His expression was indifferent as though he were only asking for an ordinary business favor.

Vera understood what he wanted. She took out a little notebook and a pen. "All right, darling. What do you want me to ask?"

He stretched his neck upward and kissed her on the lips. "Thank you. You don't know how much this means to me."

She smiled through her tears. "You know I'm the perfect secretary. Just like the old times."

He did. For many years after getting her diploma in French and German literature, Vera could not find a steady job. All she could get were odd teaching hours, language courses, and individual lessons – all badly paid. Then came their first baby. He thought they would never survive. He had just opened a company in Trieste and in Ljubljana, the new capital of democratic Slovenia. It had thrived from the start. He was hiring people on a big scale. Vera was depressed, so he hired her as his assistant. Reluctant at first, she dived into insurance policies and efficiently organized their quickly growing business. She even made a few deals on her own with the German companies Allianz and Axa. The market was hungry for new products.

However, the spouses often dragged their problems from work into their home and bedroom. Instead of making love, they fought about a rep's fee or about the achievements of a specific group leader. Their irregular office hours added extra strain in caring for their two children. They were both relieved when Vera got a position as editor in a mid-size publishing house and their work relationship ended.

"When will I need morphine injections? How do we know when it's time?"

She struggled to hide her shock. Had Adam not consider

fighting it? Haven't the doctors suggested any treatment? An operation? Chemotherapy?

"Did you get that? Good. Can they prescribe cannabis oil? It is good for pain and helps with depression."

She continued scribbling without saying a word.

"How long will I be able to walk? I mean, how long before my legs give out?"

Had the other visitors gone? Adam's questions seemed to echo in the room. But it was just the opposite. Like background noise in a movie, the cacophony of voices had never stopped.

"When can I go home? There's nothing more they can do, so there's no point in keeping me here." He had an apologetic look on his face.

She put down her pen. "Adam, I don't understand. Aren't you going to seek treatment? What about surgery? Maybe they can slow the progress." She held her breath before blurting out, "Don't you want to live?"

Her desperate cry cut through the air. The buzzing of small talk died out as though somebody had stopped the movie. Silence. They could hear the drops from the IV bag falling in the drip chamber before the liquid flowed into Adam's veins.

"It's okay, folks. Nothing can cure me better than my wife's firm hand." Adam grinned around the room.

Ever the problem solver, the fixer.

The visitors politely smiled back and continued their empty conversations. What could you really talk about around hospital beds? Even the weather outside was irrelevant since the room's temperature and humidity were regulated. The meals were as regular as the doctor's visits. The hospital's routine was more relentless than army drills.

"I'm so sorry, Adam," she stuttered.

"I just want to go home. This lousy food will kill me before the cancer does," he said, joking. Vera stayed very serious. "Vera, there's nothing they can do. I've been through check-ups. I've gone over the situation with Dr. Janek. My tumor is inoperable. The metastases have spread to the liver. They would have to cut out half of my insides to remove the cancer. Right now we just have to find a way to live with it."

"Do you think this doctor is going to tell me more than he has told you?"

"We'll see. That's often the case. Somebody in the family needs to know what's really happening."

Vera's efficiency took over. She pecked him on the cheek and stood up. "I'll wait for his office to open and come back later. So long, darling."

"Thank you," he said, closing his eyes in relief.

She dragged her feet in foggy despair down the corridor, a tunnel without light at the end. She barely knew how she arrived at the hospital cafeteria. She found a table on the terrace. A view of the streets filled with people hurrying in every direction was better than the loud music inside. All these people hurrying somewhere. Where? For how long? Who knows what cellular bomb was ticking in each of them?

"Hello, madam. What can I get you?" a waiter asked politely.

"Do you have cigarettes?"

"Yes. Which ones?"

"Oh, you do!" she blurted out.

"Of course, we do," the boy reassured her. "Why are you so surprised?"

"This is the hospital's cafeteria – that's why! Have you never heard of lung cancer?"

All of a sudden, she felt angry. The tobacco and food industry, breweries and distilleries, cosmetic and energy companies, automobile manufacturers, the entertainment business and communication giants were all offering poison for our bodies and profiting from our indulgencies. Man's thirst for pleasure deceived for a few easy bucks. Profiteers and millionaires kept on telling us how to live. Telling us what to buy to make them richer. Oh, weren't we all fools, stupid victims of their greed? Who would profit from Adam's illness?

The waiter's smile died. "I see many patients here, madam. It is not my place to tell them whether they should smoke or not. What can I get you?"

Why was she picking on him? He was just a boy. She wanted to go deep into a forest and scream the Munch scream. Get rid of the rancor inside her. Maybe hearing her own anger and angst would make her feel better.

"A cappuccino and a pack of Camel Lights. And matches, please."

When he returned, she tried to redeem herself by smiling, but his face remained stern.

"We don't sell matches. You can use my lighter."

The boy waiter could read her like an open book. Every day he witnessed the dramas of patients and relatives confronted by terminal diagnoses. He had learned to ignore their abuse. He practiced patience in the role of an angel, at once distant and near. He served them coffee, tea, and a moment of quiet compassion. In spite or because of their grim future, they needed to feel they were still part of humanity.

Vera thanked him kindly while her thoughts drifted back to Adam's questions. She inhaled deeply. She must review her notes before meeting with the specialist. The scribbled pages were a mess. She tore them out and copied the items one by one, numbering them and adding her comments. Under How long will I be able to walk? she put: walking aids, transport to the hospital, who to ask for prescription, the role of the family doctor. Her hand trembled.

A familiar voice interrupted her. "Oh, I think I had my last cigarette in high school."

She looked up. "Oh, Suzy, hi!" She got up and hugged her friend.

"Hello, Vera. What brings you here?"

Vera was reluctant to say anything. "Oh, just waiting to see a doctor."

"Anything serious?" Suzy asked, dropping her bags on an empty chair.

"Not really, I'm fine. And you, what are you doing here?"

Suzy took a cigarette out of the box and lit it. She burnt a third of it with one long drag.

In spite of the grim day, Vera had to laugh. "You haven't had a cigarette since high school? Liar!"

"At least since Lana was in high school." Suzy grinned. "What the hell! I'll have some brandy, too. This is the worst day of my life, Vera."

Concerned, Vera touched her childhood best friend's elbow. "What is it, Suzy?"

Suzy shook her head. "Mother has just been admitted. She has a malignant tumor. She has to undergo surgery."

Why didn't this come as a shock to Vera today of all days?

"I'm so sorry," she said. "How is she taking it?"

"She's always been difficult, but now you can just imagine. A monster of a mother. I'm her personal punch bag. She blames me for everything."

Vera didn't remember Suzy's mother as a monster. Victoria was a beautiful woman with a soft voice and loving attitude, although there was a strange persistence in her manner. Very different from her cold and selfish mother, whose only concern was her own well-being. Vera's prevailing memories of her parents were their constant fighting.

Like that summer afternoon when she and Suzy were six. One of the hottest days of 1971. Everybody was looking for shelter in a cool place. The two girls were playing with their dolls under the kitchen table. Suzy was gracile with green eyes, her blond hair tied in a ponytail, wearing a cute summer dress with yellow and white daisies. Vera was chubby, her eyes brown, and her hair cut to a bob with bangs. The upside-down pot look. She didn't have any pretty clothes, only hand-me-downs from older cousins. They placed a home for one doll under one chair and another under the opposite chair. Their dolls met in the middle to have tea and biscuits among the assembled toy blocks, their voices the chatter of two little girls. All of a sudden, there was a bang and a woman's cry from the bedroom. A terrible quarrel broke out seasoned with foul language. Vera froze. Her parents. Didn't they know she had Suzy over? They had no shame. Tears sprung to her eyes while Suzy swiftly collected the dolls and toys in a plastic bag. "We can play in the yard, Vera. Don't cry!" she said, heading for the door. Without a word, they left the conjugal battlefield. The expression "war of the roses" was too tame for what Vera had been through as a child.

"Well, your mom has been sad since your father's death. They loved each other very much," Vera said, pulling herself back to the present.

Her parents were so different from Suzy's. Shouts from the bedroom were their lullabies for her. She often cried herself into fitful sleep, worrying about who got hurt and what she'd find broken in the morning. Money was scarce and the damages of their fights were costly. A lamp, cups and saucers, glasses. One day Mother had to serve them dinner from a saucepan since her parents had smashed all their plates on the floor. The three of them sat around the table spooning macaroni with tomato sauce like WWII partisans.

"I need to go to the restroom," said Suzy, getting up from her chair. She had put on weight again. "I'll give my order to the waiter on the way."

Vera sighed and focused on her forthcoming meeting with the specialist. Just in case, she pulled out her phone and checked out pancreatic cancer on Wikipedia. What a nightmare. Adam was right. It was incurable. Twenty-five percent survived for one year and only five percent lived up to five years. She felt herself lose hope.

Why him?

How could she live without him?

Would he live to see his grandchild?

She donned her sunglasses to hide her tears.

"Oh my God, you're crying, Vera." Suzy came back and hugged her. Before long Vera was sobbing in her arms like a little girl.

"I've always wished I'd die before him, Suzy," she stammered.

Without replying, Suzy tightened her hug. When the waiter brought her brandy, she silently offered Vera a sip. They shared the drink as they'd always shared the joys and sorrows of their lives.

After some time, Vera told her about Adam.

"We'll get through this together, Vera," Suzy said.

Vera's nod was a passive white mask.

"Let's keep in touch. Update me on Adam's progress, and I'll update you on Mom's. We'll both have a shoulder to lean on."

"And a beer to cry in," Vera said with a faint smile.

Suzy held her hand. "I love you, Vera."

They looked at each other. Fifty years had passed since they played with dolls. Life went by as quickly as a wink of God's eye. Boyfriends, husbands, children, jobs, ups and downs.

Still, there was a glimpse of hope in their eyes.

Friendship was a river with two banks. As long as there was water, the banks remained united. Nothing could dry the flow of their love.

Her Footprints in the Grass

> A Rock, A River, A Tree
> Hosts to species long since departed...
>
> – On the Pulse of the Morning,
> the poem Maya Angelou recited at Bill Clinton's
> first inauguration on January 20, 1993

A morning like no morning before. The sky whitewashed by last night's rain, the sun still hiding behind the soft curves of the hills, foggy veils trailing over the flowers bathing in crystal dewdrops.

Victoria opened the front door and carefully took a few steps on the gravel towards the grass. Upon rising from bed and before her muscles guided her body in making the right moves, she needed a walking stick. Her eightieth birthday was years ago; these days she walked on three. What did the Sphinx ask Oedipus? What creature has one voice, but transforms from four-footed to two-footed, then to three-footed in the end? There she was – the three-footed woman. Her legs too frail to walk. One slip and she could break her hip and end up in one of those nursing homes rotting away in her own feces.

"Oh, my little sphinx, where have you been?"

Laika, her rough collie, tenderly offered her cold muzzle. She was a quiet and even-tempered dog. A real beauty with long brown and white hair that Victoria adored combing. She couldn't wish for a better companion in the wilderness she had chosen over city life.

"Laika has more sense than half of humanity," Victoria often praised her. "One day she will learn to speak."

She had found her three years ago in the forest where she was picking the first porcini mushrooms of the season. A puppy, maybe six months old, abandoned and lost. Victoria took her home where she fed and took care of her. The name of the first dog in space came to Victoria as she watched Laika's cute tail spinning around on the grass. A gift from the cosmos, a friend for life.

Laika stood patiently by her side. Victoria breathed in the rich scents of an Indian summer – roses, rosemary, sage, basil, and a pale blue hydrangea in the shade. She knew how to take care of her silent allies. Watering, pruning, fertilizing. She could chat with them while a soft breeze caressed their leaves and petals. She ran a free hand over the lavender bush in its second bloom. The distinct smell reminded her what she wanted to do. Lately, her mind wandered and slipped into oblivion so easily.

Today she wanted to walk bare feet on the grass and pick some bluets, poppies, and daisies from the unmown patch of the meadow. Bees and bumblebees found refuge there, as well as crickets and grasshoppers, and when it rained for days sometimes even tiny frogs. The flowers at her night table would be a reminder of how life vigorous was outside the hospital.

Victoria wanted to live.

Death was not an option.

She would kill the cancer in her breast. Not just cure, overcome or survive it, but destroy it.

She would not give in.

She would prove to the world she still had the warrior in her. Young people didn't know a thing about fighting. Victoria did.

She would show her daughter Suzy how it was done. The girl needed such a lesson.

She pulled her feet from her slippers and stepped on the soft green carpet. Laika observed her moves with a question in her hazel brown eyes. What was Mistress doing? Victoria closed her eyes in pleasure. The damp moss kissed the arches of her feet. She paused. The moment was so exquisite that she hesitated to shift her weight from one leg to the other. The lemony scent of crushed stems intoxicated her. It was like making love to the earth. A big smile lit Victoria's face and she could feel a tickle in her loins. It was sexy. Walking barefoot was sexy. Young people thought the old no longer knew a thing about erotic pleasures. That they no longer remembered. Oh, but they did. Old bodies could summon the ecstasy to mind during long sleepless nights. They relived legs, arms, and hair entwined on moist sheets. The scent of lovemaking was in their memory from their first time with someone to their last. The brain might succumb to dementia, but the body would still be able to feel the spasms of orgasm.

"Let's have a walk, Laika, just like old times."

The dog pricked up her ears and followed obediently.

When Victoria thought of love and sex, she thought of her husband Anton. They had met at the dancing hall. Handsome and funny, he won her over in no time. They got married a few months after a passionate love affair. Suzy was a fruit of that passion. When he died from a heart attack a decade ago, Victoria decided to follow him to his grave.

She did not do it right away. She waited a few months when her family and friends were on holiday. It was summer. She was still living in an apartment in the city. She spent most of the day leafing through old photo albums and reading long-forgotten letters. That evening she swallowed the three-month supply of sleeping pills her doctor had prescribed for her. In the heat of her decision, she forgot about her neighbor Denis, a widowed Bosnian cook who had invited her over for a dinner of stuffed peppers. When she didn't turn up at eight, he came to her door. After calling her name and ringing the bell for some time, he called the police and the ambulance. Just in time.

They pumped her stomach and saved her life. They released her from the hospital the next day. The doctors made her go to therapy, which she considered unnecessary, under threat that if she did not, they would tell Suzy about her attempted suicide. With Denis, her secret was safe. In the end, she was grateful to him. She realized how much she loved life. Every moment of it. She had portraits and photos of Anton framed and set up an altar for him in every room. Fresh flowers and scented candles reminded her of her beloved. She learned to live alone, although he was often on her mind.

One more step. The dew cooled her feet. She moved slowly, leaning on the stick, Laika in tow. When the sun came out, she picked the flowers. Now back to the house. Coffee, bread, and homemade strawberry jam. Around eleven, her old school friend Mario would take Laika with him. At noon, Suzy would come and drive her old bones to the hospital. The surgery was in two days.

When would she be back in her tiny village and her lovely house? How would Laika take her absence? The soft curves of her home, the Brkini Hills, were the only place she ever wanted to be. Snowdrops in spring, cherries in early summer, chestnuts and apples in autumn, and the bora howling around the house in winter.

The doctor said she had to stay in the hospital for two weeks.

By then, the plums would have all rot.

She should ask the neighbor's boy to pick her a basket. She could have them after the surgery and share them with her roommates and the staff.

Suddenly, her legs wavered. She had to kneel down and sit on the wet grass. Ah, what a relief! She did not slip and fall. She just needed a few moments to rest.

Upset, Laika started jumping around her, barking and howling as though a terrible accident had occurred.

"Oh, dear. It's nothing. Come here, Laika, come."

She fondled the dog's head and chest until she calmed

down. The sun greeted them from behind the trees. A rocky wall at the end of the meadow fenced off the neighboring property. She had spotted an adder between the cracks the other day. Today it was too early for the snake to bask in the sun. The first to come out was a tiny green lizard. It moved slowly, legs and tail needing the warmth to get going. Maybe she was the same. Her blood like that of a huge old lizard needed warmth before it could flow to the limbs and make them move. If she stayed in the sun for a few more minutes, she might just spring up like in the good old days when she was a little girl running after cows and sheep in the meadows.

She touched the pocket of her robe. No phone. She forgot it in the house again.

She reached for Laika, who was lying on the grass beside her, and stroke her back.

Would she call her neighbor to help her up if she had the phone with her?

She was wearing only a thin nightgown under her robe. No underwear.

Tears blurred her vision.

Old age was humiliation and disgrace.

Should she just let the cancer finish her ordeal? Death was near, knocking at the door, scratching at the windows, sliding over the walls. It was omnipresent like the air she breathed. She should embrace it like a lover, wrap her arms around it, and hold it tight to her sagging bosom forever. Why resist? Maybe the surgery and chemotherapy won't do anything, and she would die pissing in her bed, bald and without dignity. She should let go now before the medical torture started.

Was she dead or alive?

Something in between, in the twilight. Maybe she was only pretending to live.

Victoria closed her eyes, shutting out the soft autumn light, and waited for the Grim Reaper to take her. However, the wheel of the world didn't stop spinning. She stayed there for a long time, wishing hard that she would die, calling the cosmic powers to hear her plea, crying to God to grant her this one prayer.

"Look at me, Grim Reaper, embrace me and take me with you. I won't resist, I promise. I will lie like a virgin on her wedding night. The circle of my life is many times full."

Yet, her false pleas could not fool Death, the lover of all lovers.

He knew better. Victoria had to live.

"Everything about him was old except his eyes and they were the same color as the sea and were cheerful and undefeated," wrote Hemingway in his novel The Old Man and the Sea.

Her eyes were cheerful and as green as grass. Nothing could describe her better.

Her body was another story. She could not get up. She turned her wrinkled face to the sun while a breeze blew gray hair to her cheeks. She must put on some foundation to cover the ugly brown spots on her face and some makeup to enhance the faded color of her irises.

No, she wasn't giving up. Not today.

Time to start over.

"Let's move, Laika. Let's get back to the house."

Startled into action, the dog ran towards the doorway while her mistress crawled on all fours behind her. Like a ragged old turtle. At last, Victoria reached the bench and pulled herself up. Calling on Death a few minutes ago seemed so foolish. She wasn't ready to face eternity. Not now, maybe later, at some other time.

"As you see, my friend, we still have some life in us." She patted the dog lovingly.

With her back, she leaned on the large karst stones built into the wall of the house. The stones that had witnessed her whole life. A month ago, she had celebrated her eighty-third year since coming into this world, branded by Death since her first cry.

Ding-dong! Ding-dong!

In her subconscious memory, Victoria heard the church bells ringing when she first breathed in the air of this world. Of course, she did not really remember the sound. It was the narrative of her birth. Everybody in her village had their own way of telling it.

She was the fourth child and the first girl after three brothers. On the birth bed, her mother Paula was sad and disillusioned. Her husband, having returned only months ago from the Abyssinian War led by Italy against the poorly armed natives in Africa, was gravely ill. Tuberculosis. Now she had this baby upside down in her womb. Paula could hardly breathe from exhaustion, although the labor had just started.

Ding-dong! Ding-dong!

"Let's try turning this angel around," the midwife said.

She massaged Paula's belly from different angles, pressing harder and softer until the bulge under the skin showed the baby moving. Paula thought her belly would explode from the pressure. Every tissue under her skin felt stretched and hurt. Then, at last, it was over.

"It's good we caught it before it started down the birth channel. Paula, don't push. Keep breathing!"

Mother Paula obeyed, relieved that the baby was in place. The contractions told her when and how. Now that it was head down, the child seemed small.

"Maybe it's a girl," she whispered during one of the breaks.

The midwife moved a glass of water to her lips. She gulped the liquid hastily.

"Ah, the thirst. I feel like crossing a desert." Paula smiled.

The pain of the next contraction stopped her from talking.

Ding-dong! Ding-dong!

She breathed deeply. "Why these bells? Has somebody died?"

The midwife's face froze. It was not the right time to upset the woman in labor. "Don't mind it. You have a more important task ahead." She caressed Paula's forehead with a wet towel.

Hours went by before a tiny little girl let out her first cry. Paula was delighted.

"I knew it would be a girl!"

"She's as fit as a fiddle, a little frog," the midwife replied. "Rest now, my dear."

"We will call her Victoria," Mother whispered.

She nursed her daughter and they both fell asleep. When they woke up, Paula was a widow and Victoria an orphan. Her dad had passed away while she was coming into the world. The church bells were tolling for him.

Victoria was her Mom's beloved. Her brothers were much older with a ten-year gap between her and the youngest. They ignored her most of the time. No playing, no kind words, only malicious stares. She found out the reason when she started school. When she gave the teacher her name and surname as Victoria Turk, the teacher told her it was not true.

"You cannot be Turk's daughter. He only came from the war a few months before your birth. Go home and ask your mother who your father is. This school is no place for bastards."

What a mess. That a girl of five should solve an official error of the Fascist state. The following day, Mother accompanied her. She showed the teacher the birth certificate. Father was her late husband. She was baptized under the name Victoria Magdalena Turk.

"This is untrue, Paula, and you know it." However, the teacher gave in and copied down the data from the certificate.

Hell, but that was not the end of it. The teacher, a Slovenian who was having an affair with the local Fascist commander, reported the birth certificate as falsified. The old parish priest who had issued the document was interrogated, having buried the father and baptized the baby on the same day. Father Franko had heard rumors about Paula and a widower from the neighboring village, but he didn't care. The authorities bringing everything up placed Paula under a lot of pressure. She finally admitted to adultery without denouncing the true father of her daughter. The priest vanished. He was transferred. Nobody knew where. Paula was sentenced with a monetary fine so high that they had to sell a field to pay it, otherwise the Fascist authorities would incarcerate her for God knows how long. The mysterious widower disappeared and reappeared after WWII. As much as Paula's sons disliked him, he moved in with them. They lived together as a family. Unfortunately, he was a heavy drinker. The atrocities he committed on various fronts had fractured his soul beyond mending.

Victoria, the little bastard, had to endure years of public humiliation in the narrow-minded village community. She found revenge through her intelligence. At school, she excelled in all her subjects. At the age of eleven, she left home and continued at a girls' grammar school in Trieste. She was offered a stipend in Ljubljana, where she enrolled in the university and was set to graduate as a history teacher.

Then came Anton, her first love. They were together for no more than a few months when she got pregnant and had to stop her studies. Mother had warned her not to get married before she knew her future husband better and finished her studies, but Victoria knew better. She had met her soul mate and she would not let him go.

Anton was a successful party official, a man with some knowledge of economy who became a reliable manager of big state enterprises. She easily finished her studies later and found great pleasure teaching history to the kids at elementary school. After the independence, Anton still occupied various important managerial positions and had a solid income.

The property in her home village was just one of their assets. They also had an apartment in Ljubljana and a little house on the Croatian coast where she spent much of her time back when she could still drive the car.

A little bastard now owned orchards, fields, and woods.

Victoria had made it in life.

Envy was the sweetest revenge.

She would not let Death take everything away from her.

My Love, My Life, My Death

> When I die, I want your hands upon my eyes:
> I want the light and the wheat of your beloved hands
> to pass once more their cool touch over me:
> to sense the softness that changed my fate.
>
> – Pablo Neruda,
> Love Sonnet LXXXIX,
> translated by Terence Clarke

The young nurse made a face when she saw Adam's untouched lunch.

"You should eat something, Mr. Lucca. You're losing too much weight," she said in reproach.

He shook his head, tired of hearing people telling him what he should or shouldn't do.

"It's not good," she persisted.

Nothing was good if you had cancer.

Adam tried a smile. "I'm sorry, Nurse. I've never been much of an eater."

He lay down and closed his eyes. Shutting out the world. Daydreaming. Not about the future, that door would close on him soon. He was reminiscing of the past.

The eighties were the best years of his life. The music remained unrivalled to this day, full of optimism and challenges: Bon Jovi, Guns N' Roses, Queen, and Radio Luxembourg. Disco fever was in full swing. After finishing his business degree in Trieste, he received a generous stipend from Yugoslavia that made him decide to pursue law in Ljubljana. At first, he had trouble with the Slovenian language. During the communist regime, it became inflated with socialist doublespeak that could mean many different things, including dangerous anti-state propaganda. However, he quickly learned the jargon and prospered. He even had time to enjoy life. Every Saturday he went to the disco at the Skyscraper, which used to be the highest building in Ljubljana. He danced until dawn to hit songs that always arrived late in Yugoslavia. Compared to other socialist countries under the Soviet Union and behind the Iron Curtain, Yugoslavia was an open and modern country. Living in Ljubljana was fun. His two degrees got him a good job at Triglav, the biggest insurance company named after the highest mountain of the Julian Alps. He eagerly absorbed everything he could about insurance policies, investments, business growth, plus the tricks and skills needed in a new era that was silently transforming a socialist economy into liberal capitalism.

Still, Vera was the best of all. The shy girl was like a rock in the middle of a stormy sea. They met at a singer's concert in a high-school gym. She was so beautiful. Her brown eyes and chestnut hair were like an autumn wood, sparkling with summer life, shining in the colors of the sun. It was a warm evening in October, and they walked from the concert to her home for hours. They talked about this and that, mostly about her recent experience as an au pair girl in France. For four months she had looked after the children of blue bloods, counts with a chateau in Vendée. Her narrative was full of wit and gaiety. They separated when the first wisps of grey fog announced a new day about to break. They met again a few days later. Vera was performing in Euripides' The Trojan Women, a theater play set up by the Faculty of Arts French department. She played Cassandra and her acting was magnificent. Tall Vera had presence on stage. She spoke with a clear voice, her eyes shining with the pain and insanity of the wronged heroine. He was mesmerized.

Afterwards, he asked her out for a drink at the Ljubljana Castle café. Their first kiss.

She was leaning against the railing, watching the night traffic below. He moved closer as if to whisper something in her ear, and lifted the thick tendrils from her neck. He then drifted his lips up her nape to her cheek, hoping she would turn and offer him her lips. He felt her smooth white skin tense as though invisible electrical impulses had triggered something inside her. He wanted to breathe in her scent of roses and keep it in his mind forever. She seemed puzzled and uncertain in the face of passion. At last, she turned her face. They united in a long passionate kiss.

Not once did he regret the total immersion in their entwined lives.

Love carried the scents of October. Grilled chestnuts, fading roses, and the cinnamon excitement of the future.

"It's time for your medicine, Mr. Lucca." A lovely young voice cut through his thoughts.

He knew he had to take it. For the pain, for digestion, for his blood sugar, which had skyrocketed due to pancreas failure. Like a good schoolboy, he gulped the pills down, offered a finger for the blood glucose test, then lifted his sleeve for the insulin injection.

"Your sugar is stable. Good. I have something for you." She produced a plate with artistically decorated banana split. How did she know this was his favorite dessert? Tears welled up. He struggled with his emotions for a few moments. There was so much goodness in some people.

"Thank you," he stuttered at last. "Is it okay to have all this sugar?"

"It's sugar for diabetics. The cook made it for you and a few other patients. Isn't he a treasure?"

She elevated his headrest and arranged the little table so he could eat comfortably. At last, she sat on the side of his bed, sighing. "I might as well take a break while you finish."

Adam felt as if he were seeing her for the first time. Her

nametag said Barbara. She was in her twenties with short blond hair. Dark circles around her pale blue eyes evinced her fatigue. He wanted to show he cared.

"Shouldn't you be going home, Barbara? Didn't you have the morning shift?"

She shifted her weight lightly. "My colleague's little daughter is sick, so I'm replacing her."

"But somebody must be waiting for you at home."

"My boyfriend is used to my crazy work hours."

The banana split was delicious in spite of the sugar substitute. Adam considered how to show his gratitude as he spooned ice cream into his mouth.

"What's the hospital's criteria for overtime? In my company, when people work more, they get extra pay. Can I help in any way?"

She found his offer amusing. "Ah, Mr. Lucca, the hospital is the worst employer. We're seldom paid overtime. Mostly, they just expect us to be on duty."

"You could go on strike. Asking for fair wages is a legitimate demand."

"Then you wouldn't get your banana split. And if you don't get your meals, your health would deteriorate. You would starve to death, Adam."

"I don't think that's possible. Nobody can die twice."

Although morbid, the small talk made them both smile. Adam cleaned his ice cream with the biscuit and returned the plate.

"I'll bring you a second pill of Creon. With or without real sugar, ice cream is fatty."

He touched her elbow. "Thank you, Barbara, you're an angel."

She looked as though she was about to object. "Mr. Lucca…Adam, save your breath. You'll be spending more time with us in the future," she said, her tone serious.

Adam nodded and pulled the handle to lower his headrest. "I'll ask for you on your shift. It's good to be in the hands of an angel." He winked at her.

She shook her head and left the room.

Adam's young neighbor moaned, breathing out heavily. Adam knew the boy was on a high dose of morphine. A young doctor came to check on him every hour, adding an extra dose when she feared he was in too much pain. He was at the end of life.

He looked to where two men were reading, one a book, the other a newspaper. The other young occupant of the room, who could not yet be twenty, was immersed in his tablet, headphones in his ears. Watching a movie probably. The clock on the wall showed 1:30. Vera must be with Dr. Janek. He would tell her what Adam couldn't. Not in this room in front of all these people. Maybe under different circumstances he might have. Eh, he'd certainly had plenty of opportunities. Now, she would have to hear it from a stranger.

How could he chicken out?

The disease not only made him a cripple, a candidate for a quick death, but also an abominable coward.

He should tell Vera that he had reached a decision. He had studied the laws on assisted suicide very carefully. In Slovenia, anybody found guilty could go to jail. He had found the alternative. No way would he die in his own feces, without control, at the mercy of doctors, nurses, and medical care.

As a child, he had been at the mercy of strangers for many years. An orphan whose mother had abandoned him one day in the early seventies. When he found her fifteen years later, she had never explained why. Now, it was too late. She was dead and had taken the answers with her.

He was almost five when they came to the port of Trieste where Mother found a daily job at the fish factory. It had always been like this ever since he could remember – just the two of them, days on the road, no father, no home. They rented a small room at a boarding house near Piazza Ponte Rosso. The building was in decay. The moldy corners of the dimly lit corridors were cold and scary. Adam was afraid of spiders, cockroaches, and rats lurking from dark holes. There was only one toilet for twenty people at the end of the hall. He could not count then, but they were many, everyone queueing to relieve themselves in the morning. The sharp toilet stench invaded the whole building. In every room, you could smell the outrage of humanity. Mother said it was unhealthy and filthy. Unwilling to leave him alone, she enrolled him in an Italian kindergarten. The trouble was, little Adam could not speak a word of Italian.

"Sciavo, sciavo!" the children called him.

He knew it was an insult, but didn't care. Words could not hurt him. Their blows did, though. Undernourished and weak, he couldn't run away from their assaults. The teacher never intervened and seemed to side with the bullies. Adam took to hiding in various places to avoid them. He was careful to show up at the roll call. However, on the fifth day, he found a hole near the building furnace. The cellar floor wasn't very comfortable and it was dark, but it was warm and he had peace. With the furnace gently buzzing, he fell asleep.

After some time, Teacher realized he was missing. She got scared. She didn't like the little sciavo boy, but he was her responsibility. They searched the playground, all the rooms, the toilets, the attic, and the cellar. She feared he might have wandered outside the fence and gotten lost in the streets where all sorts of evil preyed – kidnapping, abuse, human trafficking. The boy had lovely blue eyes and curly blond hair. At last, the headmistress called the police while the janitor went in search of his mother. She came to fetch the boy at the usual hour. And during the havoc that soon erupted, the boy was sound asleep, dreaming of sunshine and candies.

When the janitor came to switch off the heating that evening, he found Adam.

"Oh, you!" His heavy fist struck the boy in the mouth.

Adam felt as if his milk teeth would fall out all at once. He was bleeding.

"Sciavo, the whole of Trieste is looking for you. Your teacher, your mother, the police! You little rogue!"

Adam curled into a ball to protect his face with his thin arms. He didn't understand a word of the man's furious screams, but something terrible must have happened. Where is Mommy? Then, words he had heard at the market came to mind.

"Carabinieri, carabinieri, aiuto!" he cried at the top of his lungs.

The janitor stopped. What would the headmistress say if she found the little scoundrel beaten? He turned off the heating and dragged the boy out of his hiding place to the office.

"We'll see who the police will punish for this," he hissed before dialing a number.

Adam sat on the chair, assessing the blows he'd received and wiping his tears. His stomach grumbled with hunger. He feared the man would start hitting him again.

The teacher and the headmistress arrived first, both screaming at him in Italian. At last came Mother and he jumped into her arms, crying big tears. She patted his back, sighing. "What am I to do with you?" she murmured in Slovene. In his happiness, Adam didn't detect the annoyance in her voice. For Mother, being a mother was tough, and being a single mother was beyond her capacities.

He didn't return to the kindergarten.

She told him she could not bring him with her to the fish factory.

"Why?"

She just shook her head without replying. He needed to wait somewhere while she worked. The following day, she locked him in the stinky room where they lived. He was hungry and bored most of the time.

When she came home that evening, she found the boy in tears.

The next day, she found a better solution.

She paid the watermelon merchant at the corner of the market. Gianni from Sicily was willing to look after him for a few liras. Gianni loved children. He had six at home. He transported fruit in his shabby old truck to the North. He slept in his truck, ate in a corner of the market, and washed in a restroom inside the nearby railway station. Adam didn't know how Mother found Gianni, but his hungry eyes were always on her. He must have liked her. His pile of watermelons was huge. Gianni would return home once he had sold them all.

Adam adored watermelons. He could eat a ton of them.

Sweet, sticky juice trickling down his fingers was heavenly mana he could enjoy every day.

Gianni even taught him how to spit out the seeds.

When there were no customers, they would compete on who could spit further.

Adam's world was perfect.

Every morning Mother attached a small pouch containing Adam's documents around his neck in case anything happened. Then she took him to Gianni where Adam helped arranged watermelon slices on a tray. Customers hurrying to work were encouraged to try a piece. Gianni taught him a few catchy phrases on his first day.

"Signora, per favore, provi un pezzo! Signora, provi!"

Almost every passerby, captivated by the cute blond boy, tried a bite. The sales rocketed, so Gianni started telling everybody that Adam brought him good luck. When Mother came from work in the early evening, Adam felt sorry to leave his new friend and return to their stinky hole.

One evening Mother did not show up at the usual time.

"Maybe she's late," Gianni said. "Let's get washed and find a place to eat."

They went to the station restroom together.

Gianni bought Adam a pasta dinner. Macaroni with cheese and ham. Adam had never eaten anything so good in his life.

"Eat, my boy, you deserve it. Thanks to you, I've sold most of my watermelons in a few days." He patted Adam on the cheek and emptied his glass of red wine.

In the middle of the meal, Adam started to worry about Mother looking for him while they were at the diner. He tried to explain this to Gianni who didn't understand Slovene. A waitress came to help with the translation. Gianni nodded and they quickly finished their meal.

They returned to the truck, expecting to find his mother waiting there.

There was no sign of her. No note, nothing.

Gianni shrugged his shoulders and took the boy to his makeshift bedroom among the watermelons. Adam was crying.

"We'll look for your mamma tomorrow. Don't worry, Adam. All will be fine," Gianni said to console him.

At last, the boy fell asleep in his arms.

When Mother did not appear the next morning, Gianni found a police officer and told him about the missing woman. The officer inspected the boy's documents, took notes, and promised to find her.

Piazza Ponte Rosso was particularly crowded that Friday. People from all over Communist Yugoslavia came to shop for clothes, toiletries, and food that were scarce during the nation's five-year planned economy. Jeans, leather shoes, laundry detergent, and coffee were the most in demand. Locals were shopping for fruits and vegetables for the weekend.

By noon, Gianni and Adam had sold the last watermelon.

Gianni was getting impatient.

He felt sorry for Adam, but could not bring home another mouth to feed.

Still, he couldn't leave the little boy alone.

At last, he scribbled a note and stuck it on the door of his truck. Lifting Adam onto his shoulders, he said, "Let's go for a swim!"

They walked to the Miramare beach where they enjoyed the water and the sun. Gianni tried to teach Adam to swim, but the boy was ungainly and afraid of the salty water. Every time he let him float on the surface, Adam panicked and screamed. He had never played in water.

When they returned to the market, several carabinieri were leaning against the watermelon truck. After questioning Gianni at length, they told him what they had discovered.

"She's disappeared, vanished into thin air. She didn't pay the rent. They've never heard of this woman at the fish factory. God knows how she was earning a living," the senior officer said.

Gianni shrugged his shoulders. Adam was scanning their faces, looking from one to the other, trying to understand what they were saying. He knew it was important. It was about Mother. Was Mother ill? Was she dead?

"What now?" asked Gianni.

"There's nothing you or we can do, sir. We'll take the boy to the orphanage. We've already informed them."

"Porca putana!" Gianni swore angrily. "How can she abandon her own child like this? What if I took him home with me to Sicily for a week? I can bring him back in my next haul. A sort of holiday. Maybe the woman will turn up by then."

"That's legally impossible. You could be charged with kidnapping in case she turns up in the meantime."

Adam saw tears in Gianni's eyes and panicked. "Mamma, mamma!" he cried.

"Do any of you speak Slovene? The little chap doesn't understand a word of Italian."

A young officer stepped forward and stooped to the level of the child's scared eyes. He took Adam's hands in his and explained slowly what had happened and where they would take him. He tried not to say that Adam's mother had abandoned him. He was also careful not to scare Adam more by making him suspect she had an accident, maybe a fatal one. Adam was all attention. He didn't miss a word. When the officer finished, they expected Adam to scream and cry, but he just nodded lifelessly. He understood.

Who would look after him now?

Would he ever find love?

It was his fault. Mother left him because he was a bad boy.

If anything happen to her, it would be because of him. She was never free with him around. She had to drag him from town to town. She was a slave and he was her shackles.

For years afterwards, Adam always felt guilty when thinking of his mother.

Gianni took a key ring from his pocket, the one with a metal anchor on a chain. "Adam, one day you're going to have a family and a house. Remember me and know I loved you. Many people will love you for you are a very good boy." His voice cracked as he shoved the key ring in Adam's hands. The officer translated with a trembling voice. Gianni took out his wallet and gave Adam a banknote for five thousand liras.

"Grazie, Gianni," the boy said.

"It's nothing. You earned it. You helped me sell my watermelons. Keep it safe," he replied.

The young officer explained to Adam in Slovene about the money. He would make a special note in the police report so the money didn't change hands.

Adam examined the note – the image of a handsome young man on one side and a fairy on the back. Then, he meticulously folded it and put it in the small pouch with his documents: passport, birth certificate, Yugoslav vaccination card.

His life was now in the hands of the strangers.

After fifty years, he was back at the beginning again. His fate at the mercy of strangers. But he wasn't a helpless child now. He could make decisions and was determined to have his own way.

The young man on the neighboring bed – a living skeleton of pain – gave a long anguished sigh. It was his last. His breathing stopped and eternal silence took over.

Adam pressed the red button. "Nurse Barbara, my roommate…I think he's passed on," he said hesitantly.

She hurried to the bed and checked the boy's pulse. "Poor fellow, he saved himself from more pain. He was in such agony." She softly closed his eyes and pressed another button. A young medical intern came to the room. "Philip, please call Dr. Breda.

I think our Peter is gone."

Adam sat up on his bed. "Nurse Barbara, my wife is about to come back any minute. Can I wait for her in the hall? I can drag the IV stand with me."

She could read it his face – he didn't want his wife to see death, although it was imminent. His cheeks showed more color since he had eaten the banana split.

"Sure, go ahead. Do you need help with the robe or an aide to walk with you?"

He was already up. "No, I can manage. Thank you, Barbara."

"It's my job. You don't need to thank me all the time, Mr. Lucca."

"Call me Adam, please. Thank you for being such a wonderful person. And yes, I need to say thank you every time to remind you of this."

He managed to get the tubing inside his sleeve and out of his collar. Putting on his slippers, he staggered into the hall. He felt stronger with every step he took.

Vera was already hurrying towards him.

"There's a TV room. Let's go there. They're changing one of the patients."

She made a face. He saw her repugnance and thought of the care he, too would need soon. Illness and death belonged to a different universe. He wondered what Dr. Janek had told her.

They sat in the corner. Taking a plastic bottle out of her bag, she said, "I brought you some cold water. I heard patients complaining about all the drinks being lukewarm."

"Thank you." He smiled. Vera had the gift of observation. He turned the cap and drank the content almost in one gulp.

The fresh drink revived him. Thirst was one of his enemies lately.

"So, how did it go? What did he say?"

Vera sighed. "It doesn't look good. He explained your decision not to undergo therapy. It is very unorthodox. In his way, he wanted me to persuade you to reconsider and start the chemo," she said, her voice wavering.

He took her hand in his. "Vera, we've had a wonderful life. The therapy could maybe slow the growth of the tumor for a few months, but it has so many side effects. When I studied the options, I decided to let it go."

She looked him in the eye. He had been there for her when she needed him. Many years had gone by, the images fading, yet the pain was still in her chest, suffocating her.

"I'm just trying to understand you, Adam. You know you can count on me."

"I know, darling. Please forgive me. I should have told you the moment I found out."

She smiled. "I admit it's hard to take in all this in one day. Still, I don't blame you. We must focus on what's ahead now. The time we still have together, Adam."

He kissed her on the cheek. "Thank you."

Looking away, she stared out the window. "Dr. Janek didn't give me a good impression. He seemed nervous and disorganized. Shouldn't we get a second opinion? What if he's wrong and something could still be done?"

He had expected as much. "Please don't be mad at me. I've known it for some time," he said apologetically.

"I know. He told me. Since Easter." The calmness in her voice was for show. Her confidence was shattered; he had lied to her. "You were even admitted for tests on two occasions. Your mysterious business trips."

"I'm sorry."

"I knew you were hiding something. In May, I thought you were having an affair." She gave a faint smile.

"Yeah, indeed. Only it is a he. Death."

She looked at him again.

"I wish it were a sexy young lover, not a bony old devil."

They burst into laughter. She had tears in her eyes, longing for him to tell her the whole truth at last.

"Vera, I didn't know how to cope with the situation. I went to Switzerland for a second opinion. Unfortunately, the Swiss specialists confirmed Dr. Janek's diagnosis."

"Why Switzerland? You could have found somebody closer."

He had to confess everything now. "Because once the Swiss doctors have confirmed that you're gravely ill, you can apply for assisted suicide. I got in touch with Dignitas and paid for a membership and the procedure."

Her face turned white. They had never spoken about the end of their lives. They knew death intimately, though. A tragedy buried in the past. Healthy and in their early fifties, they thought they had a future ahead. Middle age with more time for themselves. Now she would be alone. Walking from the doctor's office, she recalled all the mornings they were late for work because they had started a discussion over coffee on how to save the world. Migrants, wars, poverty, poorly paid small jobs, everything ground down to coffee dregs. Either he was telling her of a new way to insure people in case of accident or she was telling him about the new book she was editing. The space and time between them were words, phrases, observations, little things that only deep love could bring to life.

The harmony was as invisible as fairy dust, yet stronger than steel chain.

"Adam, you want to end your life."

"I'm doing it my way," he said with determined voice.

She couldn't believe what she was hearing. "What about me? What about the kids?"

"I guess we'll have to tell them."

Moving closer, she put an arm around his shoulders. "Don't you think we could at least try and fight this together?"

He shook his head. "Vera, this is bigger than us. We've already lost this battle."

"But maybe we can gain more time together," she said gently.

He saw the fear in her eyes. "We must be strong now. What else did the doctor say?"

"He didn't answer your questions directly. He said he could prescribe morphine pills for you to take regularly. As for walking, again he can't foresee how long before your legs give out, but certainly not for the next few months. That much I got out of him. It was like extracting a tooth from his mouth. I'm sorry, but I didn't get a good impression of him. He doesn't know, it depends, every patient is different." Anger crept into her voice. She needed a scapegoat.

Adam caressed her cheek gently. "Thank you, you did well. I'll try to get my discharge papers tomorrow. We should go to Switzerland as soon as we can. Can you take some time off?"

It was the peak season in publishing, just before all the major book fair events. She was bound to travel to Frankfurt and Belgrade. She dismissed all thoughts of work. "Of course, I can. You come first. Besides, I can do my editing at a hotel in the Alps."

"Good. Tell the children. Maybe not about the Swiss solution. Not yet, please."

She nodded. She knew how to organize the family. Only this time the Grim Reaper had crossed her plans.

They walked together to his bed. There was no sign of the dead boy. He saw Vera notice his absence, raising her brows in question, but didn't say anything. She tucked him in and left.

He knew she would take care of everything. He was not alone in this any longer.

What a fool he had been not to tell her earlier.

On the trail of his childhood memory, he thought of Gianni again. He was in his seventies when Adam looked him up in Sicily. Adam showed him the key ring with the anchor and proudly presented his family. Italian was his second language now, and they talked long hours about Trieste and watermelons. Gianni proudly walked them around his farm. Adam told him he had finished university, built a company, and found Mother. Gianni grinned happily, showing his tobacco-stained teeth.

"I'd always known you'd be a success, little Adam boy. You

had salesmanship written all over your angel face."

With the prayer that the nuns in the Trieste orphanage made him say at bedtime, Adam sank into sleep.

> Angel of God, my guardian dear,
> to whom His love commits me here,
> ever this day be at my side,
> to light and guard, to rule and guide.
> Amen.

The Red, Red Plains of the Karst

> New children play upon the green,
> New weary sleep below;
> And still the pensive spring returns,
> And still the punctual snow!
>
> – Emily Dickinson, New feet within my garden go

The freeway was busy, the drivers nervous. A constant flow of cars left behind the fog of Ljubljana, passing the Barje plain and ascending the karst fields of Logatec and Postojna. At the end of October, the slopes were fiery with sumac bushes shedding their last flames of the season. It was like driving through blazing hell. Reds, oranges, yellows. What passionate colors! Suzy loved sumacs even though they were useless. The shrubs were full of contrasts. In spring, they produced delicate pink flowers that seemed like smoke rising from rocky ground. In autumn, their bright colors flared through the fog and gloom of the season.

Belated passion, glowing when the season is over, thought Suzy as she sped along the freeway towards Trieste. Like Indian summer or an old woman's love.

Suzy was taking a midweek day off. Her only appointment was an early meeting with the manager of a hinge factory in Sežana about some legal issues with Ikea. With Ikea having an army of skillful lawyers, it wasn't an easy case. Still, they were on Slovenian territory where the law was on her side. For once, she wasn't dealing with inheritance issues or a divorce. Both areas were notoriously depressing, especially witnessing people who used to love each other now ready to cut each other's throat.

She turned on the radio, flipping through the stations. News, disco music, a concerto. Oh, she knew that one. Yeah, it was Beethoven's Pastoral Symphony. The soothing notes of the beginning caressed her ears.

Her business meeting had gone well since the legal disagreement was a minor one. Ikea rejected an order because of poor quality then later accepted it, but left the bill unpaid. The manager was unsure if his accountants had made an error in communication. Looking into the matter, she reassured him that she would write them and solve the misunderstanding quickly. Somebody had probably been careless. It was a common problem when it came to multinational companies.

Leaving the factory, she drove towards Divača, passing the Škocjan Caves, one of Slovenia's most visited tourist attractions. Her spirits rose as the road turned into the chestnut and oak woods that led towards little villages and orchards. It was only eleven, the sun was out, and she had a wonderful day ahead of her.

Mother had surgery a week ago and was relatively well – a bit disoriented, but in good spirits. The doctor told her she could apply for a silicone prosthesis once the scar had healed. Her question: Why would I need two boobs at my age? made him wink playfully at her. "You never know, Victoria. People fall in love in retirement homes all the time." Mother must have recounted the conversation to Suzy at least ten times. A few times on the phone, many more face to face. Like a good daughter, she listened with fresh interest every time.

Mother enjoyed being at the center of attention and getting daily visits. Lana, who was studying medicine, came with fresh fruits in the morning, while Suzy came with snacks or a magazine in the afternoon after the court had closed. Not without pride, Victoria confided to Suzy about having the most visits and gifts of all the patients in the ward. What a jungle! Did people never stop feeling competitive? Would the contest continue in the cemetery? Who got more flowers or bigger candles on All Souls' Days?

Suzy shook her head.

She wasn't any different though. Her competitive streak revealed itself in front of judges and against opposing parties as she articulated all sorts of legal mumbo jumbo.

Today, she must stop thinking of other people. It was her day off.

The Pastoral Symphony reached its peak with violins chanting the beauty of nature. "La-la-la-la-la-la…" Suzy murmured, tapping out the notes as she climbed the last curves before turning into the yard of the house. It was the first in the village, a bit isolated, but not too far from its neighbors. She turned off the engine and unlocked the front door. A tomcat meowed and rubbed up against her legs.

"Oh, look who's here!"

She opened a can of cat food before changing into outdoor clothes. With a baseball cap and garden gloves, she was ready for the gardening chores she had promised to finish before Mother came home from the hospital.

Mother was feeding half the cats in the village. Suzy never knew which, if any, belonged to her. "They earn their keep. I have no rodents in my house or garden!" she liked to say.

For her seventieth birthday, Victoria sold the comfortable Ljubljana apartment where Suzy grew up and bought a farm in the small village of her birth in Trieste's hinterland. What else was she supposed to do after her dear Anton passed away so suddenly? Cling to her daughter and her family? The rundown karst house came with over twenty acres of land, a third of which were chestnut and oak woods, another third were orchards littered with karst rocks, the rest were fertile fields. It wasn't a small plot for growing salad and parsley, but a real farmstead with a rose garden and potted plants surrounding the house. In her old age, Mother wanted to be completely self-sufficient. She ate what she produced in the fields. For meat, eggs, dairy products, and different kinds of flour, she had the local peasants to supply her. She couldn't manage to do everything alone, however. The work was too arduous without machinery. When needed, she would hire local farmhands to help her prune the cherry, apple, plum, and pear trees. The orchards were old, the trees tall and abundant, so she let her neighbor graze his sheep and goats there. In return, his tractor plowed her crop fields – potatoes, beans, cabbage, and buckwheat. It worked. Still, Victoria relied a lot on her daughter's help, especially since turning eighty. Victoria would invite Suzy's family to visit every weekend. Not without strings attached. They helped in weeding potatoes, planting beans, trimming the grass, digging, harvesting, working. No such thing as a free lunch.

It often made Suzy's husband Henry livid.

"We all have our jobs. I'm an engineer, you're a lawyer, Lana has school. We cannot support your mother's farming frenzy!"

Although a brilliant lawyer with her own firm for two decades, Suzy could never turn her mother down. She was her only family after Dad died. Every weekend she found an excuse to drag her family to the Brkini Hills and help Mother work the land. The worst part was nothing ever satisfied Victoria. Nothing Suzy did was good enough; Henry was good only for repairing electrical appliances or changing bulbs. The only person who escaped her rebuke was her granddaughter Lana. When Suzy's family returned late to their flat in Ljubljana on Sunday evenings, they were in a turmoil of quarrels. Your mother this, your mother that!

Suzy finally found a solution for her husband and daughter to enjoy coming to the Brkini Hills. After collecting a large fee from a desperate client whose company she saved from an embezzling partner, she bought two high-quality bikes and encouraged Henry and Lana to ride to the village. It took them around five to six hours. By then, much of the farmwork was done, and they could sit and enjoy lunch in the shade of the walnut tree. Everybody was happy. Henry worked on big construction sites around Slovenia during the week and was rarely home. Biking with his daughter was a way to spend quality time together. Lana loved it, thinking it was cool to share an activity with Dad.

As Mother aged, Suzy's help became imperative. Lately, she often came twice a week. Her court hearings clashed with her visits, but she made it work at the cost of having no time for rest or recreation. She scarcely found the time for shopping, usually picking the same boring grey or brown dresses and jackets, only a size bigger every time. She often worried about her weight as the numbers on the scales went up. Mother used to scold her. These days, however, she'd changed her tune. She would say, "Eat, baby, while you can" instead of "Why don't you try the Mediterranean diet for a while? You're young and pretty, you should lose a few pounds."

With echoes of Beethoven's music in her ears, Suzy loaded tools from the shed onto the wheelbarrow and headed to the field to harvest beans and weed the cabbage and brussels sprouts.

The soil under the sweet peppers was dry. The last tomatoes and eggplants of the season looked withered, too. She needed to water them thoroughly. She should probably do it first, so the sun had time to dry the leaves. Otherwise, mold would ruin the crop. The weather was warm, but the nights were cold and tiny pearls of morning dew still shone on the plants.

She went to fetch water.

Then, she harvested the vegetables, filling two crates in no time. Shiny eggplants, red tomatoes, green peppers, and yellow zucchini. She hoped Lana could give her a hand with them at home.

The pumpkins were shining at the end of the field – squash, butternuts, and Hokkaido. She would cut them and get them out of the moisture. They were already ripe. No need to let them rot.

The pole beans were difficult to work on. Too high and firmly pounded into the soil. She pulled them out one by one, at least thirty of them, tearing away the pods with their delicious seeds inside. This was the main task for today. It took a few hours before the beans were stocked in the shed for next year. She discarded the weeds and left the remaining plants at the end of the field to decay under winter snows.

Sweat was trickling down her back as she headed back to the house for a snack. A bowl of salad, cheese and crackers.

The shade under the walnut tree smelled of autumn. After the meal, Suzy stretched on the bench and dozed off. Only for half an hour.

The gentle touch of a dog's cold nose woke her.

"Oh, you're asleep!" said a rough masculine voice above her.

She opened her eyes. Laika licked her cheek. Suzy sat up. Ugh, her saliva smelled of something earthy and bad.

"Not anymore. Hello, Mario. Laika, stop it."

"She's so happy to see you. A dog's love is the only unconditional love we get in this world," he said, grinning.

He was a friend of Mother's from the house at the other side of the village, if you could call a hamlet with a bunch of houses at the top of a hill a village. Many were deserted or used as weekend homes.

"How's my school friend doing?" he asked, referring to Victoria.

"She's good, thank you," Suzy replied reluctantly.

"Did it go well? Is she awake?"

How did he know?

Mother was so adamant about keeping her cancer and surgery a secret that Suzy was stupefied. How did this aged grey man find out about it?

"Everybody wakes up in the morning." She tried to keep her voice neutral.

"Yeah, but not many of our age wake up from the anesthesia, girl." He rolled a cigarette and put it between his lips. "I know I wouldn't if they opened me up."

"Well, she did."

"Good."

She stood up and took a sip of water from the faucet, rinsing her cheek to get rid of the dog's saliva. Putting the cap on her head, she said in a firm voice, "Sorry, I have to get back to work. You know Mother. She made me a list of things to do and the sun is coming down. Thanks for looking after Laika."

"It's a pleasure. She's a good dog."

He picked up a stick from the pile of dry wood and waved it around until Laika noticed. She waited in attention. When he threw the stick, she shot off like a rocket after it.

Clearly, he didn't mean to leave Suzy alone.

"I can go with you and help in the field. You wouldn't happen to have a beer in the fridge for me, would you?"

Suzy had to smile. His idea of helping was to drink and watch. "I don't know. I can find out."

Indeed, there was a stash of beer cans in the fridge. Mother never drank beer. Wine, prosecco, sometimes a brandy, but never beer. Mario must be a more frequent guest than she thought.

"Here you go, Mario. You're better informed about what's in the fridge than I am."

"Thank you, girl. Mmmmm, nice and cold."

She gave him a brief nod and turned towards the field. She had at least another hour of work. She took a hoe and started to dig between the lines of cabbages.

Mario limped after her, coordinating his steps with the walking cane and the beer with some difficulty. He stopped a few times to adjust the cigarette dangling from his lips. Suzy was checking him out from the corner of her eye. He might slip and break something. The last thing she needed today was to rescue an old man. Did he live with anybody?

"How are you, Mario? Are you alone during the week?"

He looked puzzled. "No, I have Laika with me."

"I meant human company? Do you live alone?"

"Yes, ever since."

"Where's your family?"

He shook his head. "You know nothing about me, eh?"

Suzy dug deeper. "Sorry, Mother is not a chatty person."

"Nothing about us either?"

"Who do you mean by us?"

He grinned, display his yellowish teeth. "Your mother and me, we go a long way back. Long, long way, before you were even a thought in her head."

"How long?"

"Since she was born. I'm three years older. That long enough?"

Suzy straightened. "What were you and Mother – sandbox sweethearts?"

He burst into a fit of laughter. His cigarette fell on the grass. "Lovers, lovers, we were lovers, girl. Friends and lovers. A brother and a sister. Inseparable. We were everything to each other." He collapsed into melancholy.

Suzy drew closer. How interesting. "I'm sorry. I didn't know that. They seemed a perfect match, Mom and Dad. She never spoke of you." She touched his elbow.

Getting his feelings under control, he said, "We've been sweethearts since we were small. She had it tough, my little Victoria. She was born on the day the husband of her mother, your nonna, died. Can you imagine? Nonna was pushing a new life into the world while they took her husband to the grave."

"Why do you say 'the husband of her mother'? He was my nonno. Yeah, I heard the story," she replied with some grumpiness.

"Suzy, Nonno was unlikely your grandfather. It was another man. A relative of the aunts who used to live in this very house. He used to help Nonna work the farm while her husband was away at war. People gossiped. We all knew. When your mother was born, the poor devil drew the hatred and prejudices of our village on himself. Everybody treated her like a bastard. They cursed, beat, and insulted her. She was in tears most of her young age," he said sadly.

Mother never spoke of her childhood. On principle, she was close-lipped about her family life and kept her school years in Trieste a secret.

"But Nonna and her brothers, my uncles loved her." I tried to find some shimmer of light in her past.

"Nonna did, her brothers didn't. Have you seen your dear uncles around? Have you even met them?"

It was true. Before Mother bought the house, they had never visited the village. Later, they had very little contact. She barely knew her cousins.

"I loved her, Suzy. I loved her more than my life," he said serenely.

She saw tears gather in his blurred brown eyes. "You still love her, don't you, Mario?"

"I do. I'm not ashamed to admit it. Love is a miracle given by nature to help us endure the pains of the world."

Suzy felt the urgency in his trembling voice to bare his soul to her. Stop digging and weeding. She gathered her tools and loaded them onto the wheelbarrow.

"Let's go back to the house, Mario. We can sit down and talk. Would you like a cup of coffee?"

He nodded and followed her awkwardly. Bringing coffee and biscuits into the shade, she picked up where they'd left off.

"What happened? Why didn't you and Mother stay together?"

"My mother – that's what happened. She couldn't stand the thought of us together. Her perfect son and the little bastard. In her eyes, Victoria was a daughter of a puttana, a whore."

"And you obeyed, like a true mamma's boy." Suzy couldn't help being cynical.

"You don't understand. My dad fell at the front, fighting in the Italian army. We were alone. When I told Mother I wanted to go to Trieste and get an education, she fell gravely ill. When I left for a few weeks to join Victoria in Trieste where she was at a girls' boarding school, my mother attempted suicide. I was seventeen at the time. I came back and never left the village. Your mother didn't want to return to the place of her suffering. We parted ways." His voice trembled. "We understood each other. So deep was our love. She met and fell in love with your dad. I couldn't love another."

"Emotional blackmail. Your mother must have been a dreadful woman to manipulate you like that. Don't you have brothers or sisters?"

"No, I was an only child. The only son. I don't know if I could've lived with the burden had my mother succeeded in killing herself."

Suzy poured him some coffee and opened a jar of cookies. "Oooh, coconut vol-au-vents – the ones I love."

"Your mother made them. She must know you love them."

Coffee and cookies soon returned some color in his wrinkled cheeks. "Maybe I shouldn't have told you all this. Your mother wouldn't approve."

"No, she wouldn't."

He looked at her apologetically. "Let's not tell her then. There's no need for her to know."

"I agree. I'm glad you told me though." Suzy tried to smile. "Maybe I should have asked her about her younger days. I guess digging up secrets isn't my forte."

He touched her elbow. "You must talk to her soon before it's too late."

She nodded absentmindedly.

And I'll regret it for the rest of my life. She looked in the distance where purple clouds played with the last rays of the sun like a flock of disobedient sheep fleeing their shepherd.

He put both palms on the table decidedly. "Now please, Suzy, tell me everything – from the moment she was admitted to the last time you saw her. How's her room? The food? The doctors treating her? Everything you can think of."

If they were such friends as he claimed, why didn't Mother talk to him on the phone? Why didn't he just visit her? Suzy said, "Don't you have a phone? Haven't she called you?"

"Only once, briefly. Just to state the facts. They've cut her up, she's still alive, that sort of thing."

Suzy shook her head. She knew Mother. All the fuss she made was to give the impression she didn't want any fuss. Had Mario called every day, it might have thawed her feelings for him. Or not. Maybe she wouldn't pick up the phone, which would drive him crazy.

"Doesn't she want to know how Laika is? She adores that dog."

"She would sooner ask after her than me. But she knows Laika is fine with me." He fell silent, waiting for Suzy to give him the rundown.

"Well, she's the queen of the ward. It's a wonder she hasn't summoned you to visit her. She could present you as her admirer. Imagine the stir it would cause."

"I guess she doesn't look her best in a hospital gown."

How well he knew her.

"Well, that's true. Let me start from the beginning then."

Suzy told him everything – all the complaints and objections that accompanied every step of the way. Mother's outbursts of anger always went through her like through a lightning rod. Mario listened attentively. By the time she finished, Suzy felt almost sorry for him.

When she fell silent, he said, "You understand me. You're the same. I guess your husband and daughter aren't happy watching you wreck yourself over Mother, her garden, her field. What else does she want you to do? I can get a village lad to finish all this tomorrow. You're a lawyer, you shouldn't be breaking your back to work the earth."

"I still need to loosen the soil around cabbages and brussels sprouts, then shell the beans."

"Just leave the beans under the shed roof to dry and I'll do it. Go home and relax. Go to the cinema. Don't you city folks go to the cinema?"

"Sometimes we do." She smiled gratefully.

"Take your husband with you. It'll cheer him up."

"He's okay, my Henry. He's working at a building site in Austria now. Just coming home for the weekends."

"Oh, then just go alone or with a friend. Do you have a friend?"

"I do." Suzy thought of Vera and decided she would call her from the car. Maybe they could preserve the vegetables together and have a glass of wine afterwards. Then, she remembered Adam and winced.

"When is Victoria coming home?"

"I'm not sure. In a week or so."

He took out his cell phone – an old model with huge keys. "Can I call you sometimes?"

"Yes, of course." Suzy went into the house and came back with her smartphone. "What's your number? I'll ring you up and you can save the number in your contact list."

They agreed for her to return in a few days. The plums would have ripened by then. She would bring Lana and Henry along to help with the harvest. She would leave some to dry on racks in the attic, others she would make into delicious jams and marmalades.

The pink and crimson sky competed with the reds of the sumacs as she drove back to Ljubljana. Along the way, she called her friend. It took Vera a long time before she picked up.

"Hello, Vera. How are you?" "We're good. Just discussing dinner tonight. Adam doesn't feel like going out, and I'm not exactly good at cooking," she replied.

"If you don't mind my company, I'd love to come by and make something for the three of us. I have three crates of Mother's veggies in my trunk. We can eat some and pickle the rest for winter. Lana could come along to help, too."

Vera sounded genuinely relieved. "Sounds terrific. What else do you need? I can run to the store."

They settled for vegetable lasagna, Chardonnay, and some pickle jars.

By the time Suzy ended the call, the sun had set behind the autumn gold of the woods.

Friendship is the best of loves.

Friends in Misery

> Everyone that flatters thee
> Is no friend in misery.
> Words are easy, like the wind;
> Faithful friends are hard to find…
>
> – William Shakespeare, As it fell upon a day

The vast kitchen in Vera's house echoed with laughter and merry conversation. Lana was making the vegetable lasagna with plenty of cheese, butter, eggs, and fresh béchamel sauce, while Vera and Suzy cleaned the vegetables for winter pickles on the kitchen table. Thick tomato sauce with lots of garlic and basil, eggplants in olive oil with thyme and rosemary, green peppers in vinegar.

Adam filled the women's glasses with sweet wine. "Lana, do you want a sip of last year's Kupljen Chardonnay?"

"Thank you, Adam, but no. Judging by the amount of drinking going on here, I'll have to drive Mom home." She glanced at Suzy and Vera laughing like two silly teenagers.

Adam smiled. Stepping out onto the terrace, he turned on the outdoor lights. The garden came to life with every shade of green and orange brought about by falling autumn leaves. Droplets of evening dew gave the impression of God spreading a carpet of pearls down the gentle slope of the meadow. The gardener had trimmed the common boxwood, the juniper, and the Japanese maple in the art of bonsai, each level expressing man's desire to reach higher into the clouds, closer to the gods. In the corner, the lights revealed a covered swimming pool with a sauna and a jacuzzi where their family of four once sought recreation. Now, only Vera and Adam enjoyed it on lazy Sunday mornings when they found quiet consolation in just being together. "I love this woman with whom I can spend hours in silence and harmony", thought Adam as he stepped back inside.

"Let them enjoy themselves. We're sober, Lana, and in charge." He lifted two glasses of water. "Cheers, Lana."

"I don't know why you insist on staying sober, Adam." Lana added some tomato sauce to the eggplant filling. "You're not going anywhere tonight. You can join the hippy club over there," she said, motioning to Vera who was whispering something to Suzy's ear.

Adam shook his head. "I don't feel like drinking. I have an important appointment tomorrow. Holding supervisory board."

Lana gave a start. "Oh, that reminds me. Dad called. I must tell Mom." She turned off the heat and approached the kitchen table.

Suzy was telling one of her court stories. Without pausing, she put an arm around Lana's shoulder. It was about a well-known Slovenian CEO who blamed his wife after he had stolen the humanitarian aid fund from his company. She was demanding a new Mercedes convertible and he didn't know where to get the money for it. The company owner fired and sued him for such a despicable act. In defense, the accused asked the middle-aged judge what he would have done in his place. The judge looked at him sternly, saying, "I'd return the money first, pay the legal fees, then divorce my wife." The funny thing was, in the course of two months, all this happened.

Lana waited until Suzy finished, then said, "Mom, Dad called just before. He's coming home on Saturday. Said he has a late meeting scheduled for Friday."

Adam and Vera exchanged looks. Who would hold a meeting on Friday evening?

Suzy noticed the shadow passing across Vera's face. "What? A meeting is a meeting. Friday or Monday – what difference does it make? I don't like Henry driving tired at night just to be home on Friday. Maybe I'll take advantage of his absence and go to the theater. Besides, it's not the first time. His Austrian partner obviously has no family life." Her words hovered in the air together with the vapors from the vinegar cooking on the stove with bay leaf, black peppercorns, coriander, salt, and sugar. The acid and bitter vapors of suspicion.

Adam turned his back. He hated impropriety. He knew better. In business, gossip travelled faster than high-speed internet. Henry's so-called Austrian partner, who was keeping him on Friday nights, had long chestnut hair, a voluptuous body, and irresistible sex appeal. Her name was Tina and she was a well-known interpreter in several languages. She translated contracts, statements of work, building specifications, bills of quantities, and other documents necessary in construction projects. She was strict with language use, but loose in manners. Single and daring, always on the hunt for the right man. A decade younger than Suzy. Adam knew her rather well. She had worked for his company when the new headquarters in Austria was being built. She plied her wiles on him, too. When he didn't respond in kind, she settled for the architect supervising the site. That kind of a woman. Henry was a fool.

Vera said, "I can't imagine anybody in publishing working on Friday evenings. Hell would freeze over sooner."

Struck by the unspoken tension in the air, Suzy tried to make eye contact with Adam and Vera. In vain. A bottle of wine and an eggplant skin absorbed their attention. Finally, she shrugged her shoulders.

"We haven't any reason not to believe Daddy, have we, Lana?" She turned to her daughter for support.

Lana nodded reassuringly. Old people were so paranoid. Always seeing the dark side of everything.

Vera felt torn. What was right or wrong? Should she tell

her friend about her husband's infidelity? Was that true friendship?

Not in front of her daughter, of course.

They had always tried to be honest with each other. Phillip Pilič, that boy back in high school. They both fell head over heels in love with him. A gorgeous basketball hero. Dark with chocolate eyes and honey-colored hair. Tall as a mountain. Kind and funny. Suzy noticed Vera getting breathless around him.

"Vera, he's all yours if you want him," she said one day as they were exploring shops for the season's latest trends – a difficult undertaking in Communist Yugoslavia where goods were scarce. Things like coffee, laundry detergent, and bananas were sporadic commodities, much less jeans and designer clothes.

"Oh, it's all right, Suzy. If he likes you better, I'll survive."

Fact was, he couldn't seem to decide whom he liked better, so he kept hanging out with both of them. Suzy decided to avoid him, thus making Phillip's decision easy: Vera. They became an item, but it didn't last. Phillip was headed for America to pursue a career in professional sports. For a boy of his age, it was strange that he never tried anything sexual with Vera. He also constantly asked about Suzy: "Why isn't she coming with us?" Vera wanted to scream in his face, "Because we're a couple, you dummy!" In time, things cooled off between them and love was over before it even began. Phillip became a code word for anything Vera and Suzy both wanted.

Honesty is the essence of friendship.

Sometimes, though, honesty could be the end of it.

What if the rumors were wrong and Henry really had work to do on Friday evenings? He was handling a very complex project. Building a tunnel through an Alpine mountain meant dealing with avalanches, snows, and brittle terrain. After heavy rains, water had gushed into the shaft and flooded the site, destroying some of the machinery. It was pure luck that nobody was around at that moment. The accident was in the papers. Maybe Fridays were for recaps and planning. Maybe Henry was faithful, after all.

Vera hesitated. What would it do to Suzy? Despite her tough job as a lawyer and her mother being in the hospital, Suzy managed to remain cheerful and positive. Rumors of Henry's infidelity would devastate her. Vera couldn't bear to see her friend in pain.

Sensitivity is the glue of friendship.

She wouldn't say anything, at least not until she knew for sure.

"Adam!" cried Lana, breaking into Vera's thoughts.

Adam's eyes were closed, his face crumpled in pain, white as snow.

Vera jumped to her feet. "Adam, what do you need?"

In between harsh breaths, he said, "Medicine...my night stand drawer...please."

Vera rushed to the second floor. He leaned on the counter while Suzy brought a chair closer. He sat down. A minute later, Vera was back with the pills she had never seen before. Adam swallowed two capsules. He leaned back, all three women gathered around waiting for the medicine to take effect. Vera read the label: Targinact. Morphine pills? She had seen Adam taking cannabis oil and some digestive pills called Kreon. He was getting worse.

Suzy was nearly in tears. Vera feared she would give away that she knew. She caught Suzy's eye and shook her head. Don't show that you know!

Seeing the look that passed between them, Lana said, "What's wrong with Adam? I'll call an ambulance." She pulled out her phone.

Adam raised a hand. Unable to speak, he pointed at Vera. She read his thoughts. "Lana, it's just his stomach. The pills are for gastritis. Adam's been having some painful attacks lately. It usually passes in half an hour or so. Let's move him over to the sofa," she said, cursing the vast distance between the kitchen and their living room.

Lana and Suzy were supporting Adam, who could barely move his feet. They were able to half-carry him.

Vera fetched a pillow and a blanket. "Do you need anything else, darling?"

Adam shook his head.

They left the room, closing the door behind them.

The evening's cheerfulness was gone.

"Cancer is stigma!" Suzy thought. "Once people know you have it, they look at you as if you're a walking dead," said Mother. Adam was in the same boat. And Vera was more worried about Suzy betraying that she knew their secret than Adam's suffering.

What kind of world was this?

Friendship reduced to deceit and lies.

A carnival of sad clowns at the mercy of some wrongly divided cells.

Return to Life

> I felt a Funeral, in my Brain,
> And Mourners to and fro,
> Kept treading – treading – till it seemed
> That Sense was breaking through –
>
> > – Emily Dickinson, I felt a Funeral, in my Brain

The pink sheen of the sunset invaded her pupils as she awakened from the anesthesia. Myriad silver needles of light piercing her brain. She wasn't ready yet. Still, she continued to regain consciousness and couldn't resist reality any longer. For a moment, she didn't know where she was. Was this heaven?

"Mrs. Victoria Jug, can you hear me?" said a soft voice.

She tried to open her eyes, but her lids were as heavy as stones. She struggled to cross the river Styx. Did they put a coin in her mouth to bribe the ferryman Charon? They did not. There was no need, for she was on her way back to the world she adored. Blessed life! She was here and breathing. Joy flooded her body with warmth, tickling her skin like the silken hands of cherubim. I'm alive! I'm alive! In a few days, maybe weeks, she would return to her autumnal heaven in the Brkini Hills where they'd roast chestnuts on the old iron stove. Who? She and her friend. His name evaded her.

"Mrs. Jug, please, open your eyes now!"

Victoria hated being ordered about. She would not stand for any of it. She fluttered with her eyelids and shook her head.

"Oh yes, Mrs. Jug. Here's somebody you want to see. Wake up! Now!"

The pleasant voice of a young woman made her pause. Light seemed to explode throughout her brain. After a few moments, she felt her eyes adjust.

"Oh, it's you, Suzy, my darling angel! So glad I am not in heaven! Of course, dear God doesn't want me with him."

The two women at her bedside laughed gently.

"Mother, the Devil may take you one day if you keep demeaning God's way," Suzy said, caressing Victoria's cheek with her palm. The touch was warm and smooth as silk. She knew that touch, the miraculous hands of her daughter.

"Maybe we don't need to ask you about the date and place of your birth. You seem quite yourself, Mrs. Victoria Jug," the nurse said, nodding in approval.

"You could try, but I wouldn't tell you."

"Are you in any pain?"

"Not really. Probably because I lost a breast on my way back." Victoria's heart was bursting with joy. She wanted to entertain and embrace the world.

"We'll get you a new one – don't you worry. Use the red button if you need me," the nurse said as she stepped away to look at the other patient in the intensive care room.

Suzy bent over her mother and kissed her cheek. "They say I have to leave and let you rest now, Mommy."

"Oh, don't go just yet, my dear. I'll get bored to death." Victoria chuckled, visibly happy.

"God, Mom, you're impossible. I'll stay just a few more minutes." Suzy brought a chair close to the bed and held her mother's hand.

"Do you have today's paper, Suzy?"

"No, but I can look up the news on my phone. What do you want to know?"

"Read me some crap about President Trump and Angela Merkel. Only politicians are more brain dead than I've been during my anesthetic journey."

Suzy shook her head, grinning. "Okay, I'm searching."

"How long was I asleep?"

She tapped a link on the touch screen. "One day and a half. They were worried you wouldn't wake up easily."

"Were you here the whole time?"

"No, I had to be in court this morning. They finished the surgery around noon yesterday. When I called the front desk, they told me everything was fine and I should wait until today. They texted me just now to come over as soon as I can. It is good for patients to see a familiar face when waking up from the anesthesia."

"I wish I knew what dreams I had in my sleep of death."

Tears came into Suzy's eyes. It had occurred to her that Mother was at risk with general anesthesia. However, death was not an option. She mumbled, "They don't need to ask you about your date of birth if you're making allusions to Hamlet."

Then, she found an article about German Chancellor Angela Merkel's visit to President Donald Trump at the White House. When she tried to show the footage of the handshake Trump refused, she found Mother sound asleep.

A few days later, Victoria was transferred to the inpatient ward. The room was crowded with six beds and visitors hanging around at all times. With no peace to be had, Victoria was eager to get out of the hospital.

Although her recovery from the anesthesia had been spectacular, she didn't feel well. She could sense her memory fading. With age, it was natural to be forgetful and for the mind to become putty. However, her grip on reality was fuzzy, blotted with empty spaces with no associations. Black holes of time. She wasn't like this before. It was frightening how she couldn't remember simple everyday things. Like the name of that male friend from her village. Was he important to her? What the hell was his name? Even the name of her village. She was terrified that she couldn't remember the name of her dog. Was it Sputnik? Simple things like what she had for lunch. The moment they took away the plate, a black hole replaced the memory.

There was a bookmark in the middle The Lake, a new novel by aspiring Slovenian crime writer Tadej Golob. Yet the characters and story line – another black hole. She was sinking into dementia. It was the worst of all deaths when the mind began to go.

"You are the chosen one. You will not die!"

Victoria raised her head. It was a miracle that for once, all the beds were empty, save for Marina, another patient in the corner of the ward. A middle-aged man was sitting at her bedside. Terminal lung cancer. Victoria had overheard it from the doctor and the nurse as they were injecting morphine to alleviate Marina's pain.

She could only see the man's back. He was short and overweight, dressed in shabby, bedraggled clothes. Victoria pricked up her ears for his sales pitch.

"My drops won't only alleviate your pain, Marina, they'll heal your cancer. It's a pure and natural product."

The man must have felt Victoria's stare, for he turned around to reveal a greyish face with pig eyes, a receding hairline, and a protruding belly that looked as though it would rip apart his blue-and-yellow checked shirt any minute. His light eyes flashed with the flicker of insanity.

What was this man doing in their ward?

"What are the ingredients? It's all in Latin," Marina said feebly. Victoria felt so sorry for the young farmer's wife from Notranjska that she even asked God to take her instead of this brave mother of three, her youngest child being only seven. When her family came to visit, Victoria could see the husband was already half-broken by the atrocity of the disease. Marina was a gentle and simple woman. Everybody in the ward loved her.

The man resumed his sales pitch. "Only medicinal herbs: common centaury, cumin, aniseed, garden angelica, plus my special formula, my wonderful invention, which has helped hundreds of people like you."

"How much does it cost?" A trace of hope crept in Marina's

voice. If she took the magic potion, she could get well and be with her children. Hope is the last to die.

"220 euros. I think you'll need only two bottles of it," he said in a matter-of-fact voice.

Of course, thought Victoria, the woman would be dead before she could finish the second bottle. What a creep to prey on an innocent terminal patient. Where is security?

Still, she hesitated to intervene. She didn't want to cause a stir in the room.

"That's a lot of money," Marina said wearily.

"I know, but just think, Marina – you could get well and return to working the farm as fit as a fiddle. Think of your children! Curavit is based on the miraculous success of immunotherapy in cancer treatment. Five drops a day can strengthen your immune system, which in turn will be able to fight the cancer. Your body will virtually consume the tumors and the metastases."

Victoria wasn't going to stand by while this charlatan scammed five hundred euros from an afflicted family for nothing. "Wishful thinking, Mr. – sorry, I didn't get your name?"

"Oh, hello there" – he threw a shrewd look at the chart on the side of her bed – "Victoria. What a wonderful name! I'm Dr. Kramar, herbalist and inventor." Approaching her, he offered his right hand to shake.

Victoria ignored it. No way she would touch every shit that came her way. "What do you have there, Mr. Kramar?"

"It's called Curavit, medicinal drops that have cured cancer in some cases. Why give up? This vicious disease is not the reason to condemn yourself to death."

Victoria sighed. "Nobody wants to die. Unfortunately, the doctors can't always help the patient. Sometimes surgeries, chemotherapies, and radiation are all in vain. I've read about new treatments for cancer, like proton therapy and carbon-ion therapy." She looked at Marina, hoping to talk some reason into her.

However, she could not keep Marina from buying hope.

Wishes and dreams of health lingered in the sickly sour air as false and thin as vapors on a summer morning.

"Oh, victorious Victoria," the man said in a cloying voice, "such therapies damage your body. They do not enhance its performance but weaken it to the point that you die from the side effects rather than from the cancer itself. Curavit, on the other hand, raises your immune system and makes it fight for your life."

Too weak to sit up, Marina lay on her side, observing their exchange. Her eyes were shining like stars on a winter night.

"Mr. Kramar – "

He cut her off. "Doctor, if you please, Victoria."

"Oh, do you work for the hospital?"

He smiled condescendingly. "Of course not."

"But you do have a medical degree, don't you?"

He shook his head. "A medical degree would have prevented me from being a freethinker and inventing something so miraculous. I'm a naturopath, Victoria, a healer. I have thousands of followers on Facebook alone, many more on Instagram, Twitter, and other social media. Hundreds of people attend my presentations and workshops. Everyone's health is my personal goal and vocation," he said with an indulgent voice, his face sympathetic to her ignorance.

Did he take her for an idiot?

Inside Victoria's chest, a fury was building up, making her surgery wound swell with pain, yet she knew she had to be patient to defeat the swindler with his own words.

"I see. So you don't have any medical knowledge apart from what you acquired as a layman. Internet and Wikipedia were your teachers, if I understand correctly," she said pointedly.

With some agitation, he replied, "Well, I devoted many years to study before developing my formula. Curavit is the product of thorough research, Victoria."

"Has it been registered with the authorities? Is it on the list of JAZMP, the Agency for Medicinal Products and Medical Devices of the Republic of Slovenia?"

"No, it's only a nutritional supplement for the cures." He gave her a benevolent smile.

"Well, it should be tested and analyzed first. How else can we trust this Curavit? It could worsen one's condition and cause more pain."

He stared at her as though she were insane. "I assure you, Victoria, I'm more trustworthy than all these doctors here. They're all corrupt. They make money on your illness. A lot of money. Can you imagine how much your chemotherapy costs each month?"

"I'm not receiving chemotherapy."

"But you will. Everybody does eventually."

Victoria felt disarmed in face of his insolence.

"Several thousand euros – that's what your health insurance will be paying. Believe me, the doctors get a fat slice of that pie. That's why they prescribe all the expensive therapies. They get rich on your suffering." Outrage had turned his face purple. Going over to the sink, he poured himself a glass of water. "Just follow the money and you'll see who wants to cure you and why."

Look who's talking! Victoria had had enough of this vile man. Who let him wander freely in the wards?

"You said it! Follow the money, indeed," Victoria said sharply. "You're only after money, aren't you? You want to charge five hundred euros for your pack of lies to my friend who's in pain. You think I don't see through you? I'm calling the nurse." She pressed the red emergency button. "There must be security in this hospital. You better leave before they throw you out."

He stared at her as though seeing a ghost. He'd never run into anybody like her. He could see that Victoria meant business. Quickly, he packed his things.

"You'll regret this, you old bat! You will be begging me for Curavit when you're dying and in pain!" he said, saliva spraying out of his mouth. Sweat was dripping down his red cheek.

Victoria could smell his foul breath and turned away in disgust.

On his way out, Marina grabbed him by the sleeve. "Here, it's all I have – two hundred," she pleaded.

Grabbing the money, he tossed a bottle in her lap.

"Thief! Thief! Stop that thief!" cried Victoria when the nurse came.

Marina was sobbing, her last straw of life broken and burnt.

While Victoria explained what happened, the man had long disappeared. The nurse asked Marina for the bottle so she could send it to laboratory to check for harmful substances. If it deemed safe, the nurse promised to return it and Marina could take the drops as a supplement for her therapy.

"He only pretended to throw something in my lap. There's nothing. I don't have the medicine," Marina said.

"What a dirtbag! We have security cameras at the entrance. I'll notify the police so they can track him down. What's his name again?"

"Kramar," replied Victoria darkly. "You really should notify the police. And alert the front desk. They can't let just anybody wander into the wards. This is unacceptable."

"He probably lied and pretended to be the relative of a patient. I'm so sorry."

When the nurse left, a gloomy silence filled the room. The heart is the last to go, but today it was the heart that abandoned all hope.

"Marina, let me pay for your medicine. Nobody needs to know." Victoria took two bills from her purse and staggered towards Marina's bed.

"Thank you, but I don't take charity," she replied in a toneless voice.

"Please, take this as a present from me. Your husband can buy something nice for the kids."

"You have it easy. In spite of your age, your cancer is curable. You still have some life ahead while I...I'm dying." She buried her face in the pillow.

Victoria took her hand. "I'm really sorry, Marina. I shouldn't have meddled. Please let me make it up to you." She put the money in the drawer.

The other patients who had left for the cafeteria to chat with their visitors returned to the room.

"What happened here? You look like you've been visited by the Ten Plagues," said the middle-aged company owner and a heavy smoker in spite of the liver cancer.

Victoria returned to her bed and sank onto the sheets. "There's only one plague in this room – and we all have it!"

Family Gathering

> But all of the things that belong to the day
> Cuddle to sleep to be out of her way;
> And flowers and children close their eyes
> Till up in the morning the sun shall arise.
>
> – Robert Louis Stevenson, The Moon

The front door slammed and bags hit the floor.

"Hello. Anybody home?"

Sarah happily kicked off her shoes. These days her feet ached no matter what she wore. Always tired and heavy. She must have gained too much weight in her pregnancy. A dozen more weeks and a new life would begin.

She went to the kitchen and poured herself a large glass of water. She checked the garden to see if her parents were there. Nobody. She was alone in the house. She dialed Mother.

"Hi, Mom. Where are you? Where's Dad? Shouldn't he be resting?"

There was an awkward silence on the line. Then, Vera replied, "He felt better today so he went to settle some things at the company. He called in the supervisory board to allocate tasks and responsibilities in his absence."

What a euphemism for the fact that Dad was going to die. Death is a permanent form of absence. Sarah felt resentment towards her mother. Her heartless, lifeless attitude.

"And you let him go? You guys are unbelievable. First, you say nothing for months about the illness that's going to change our lives. Then you act as if nothing's changed at all. Where are you, Mom?"

Vera sighed. Tensions had always dominated her relationship with her daughter. Sarah's character was like Adam's. Unless she had control over the board game, she did not play.

"Please, Sarah, I told you last night that I just found out about Dad's situation. He kept me in the dark, too. I'm at work now – a few more meetings – but I'm almost done. I'll be home in an hour."

"I took the day off to come to Ljubljana," Sarah said with some reproach.

"Thank you, darling. It won't be in vain, I promise. Just relax and take a nap."

"All right, Mom. See you." Sarah gave in. She was obviously the only idiot who truly cared for Dad and the family. A kick in her belly reminded her to just sit down and enjoy the peace and quiet.

"I'll be back in an hour. We'll cook together. Bye!"

Sarah hung up. She took the remote to play some music. Grieg's "Morning" filled the sunlit room with warm optimism, reflecting the colors of the autumn leaves changing the garden in the shades of fire. It kindled hope.

"Maybe things aren't so bad and something could still be done."

When Mother called last night, it was nightmare. Dad had always been so strong and healthy. He kept fit and loved life, always facing challenges with confidence. Of course, he worked very hard. When she opted to study business at Maribor University, Dad was in the seventh heaven. He bought her an apartment in the city center with a charming view of the river Drava. She was bound to continue the family legacy and take over the insurance and financial empire he had built in the region.

Nevertheless, Sarah wanted to make her own way. Just pursuing her studies seemed too easy, so she found a part-time job at a local bank. Dad wanted her to work at one of his companies instead, but she was stubborn. It was her life and she was free to choose her path.

Then, in her third year, at the age of twenty-one, she got pregnant.

Goodbye freedom, goodbye free will. She loved Boris, but it was too much and too soon. Five years her senior, he had a good job as a software engineer in Graz and commuted every day across the border to Austria. She had ambitions, wanted to travel the world and enjoy life. It was too early to start a family. They spent long evenings together, considering what to do. She hadn't even spoken with her parents during the week she was trying to decide. Now she was angry they hadn't shared Dad's illness with her.

Double standards were easy to adopt when you considered yourself different from others.

It was a glorious spring day when she went to the clinic. Despite her agony, despite Boris's tender attempts to persuades her to get married and make it as a couple, despite his commitment to help her with her studies and career, despite his disappointment when she said no, and despite the pro-life ladies praying for unborn babies outside the clinic. She got ready, took off her clothes, and opened the door to the examination room. The freshly mopped linoleum floor smelled of citrus and something artificial. The operating theater where they would revert her into one instead of two was lit like a stage. Dust motes danced in the air, playing in the rays of the strong lamp. Her baby was now about an inch long and weighed a gram; it had internal organs and a brain. Its heart, the organ for receiving and giving love, would begin to beat any day now. Would it have fingers and legs? Would its face look like hers one day? She glanced at a white bucket in the corner of the room. Its contents showed shades of dark red. Women, strangers in their everyday life, walked out of the clinic, while their embryos stayed clumped together for eternity, rotting in a bucket. Maybe she was imagining all this. It was just a bucket. Yet something broke inside her and tears streamed from her eyes. Life. An image of a toothless baby smiling from ear to ear. Why would she get rid of it? She was loved, healthy, and rich. She decided to keep her child. Not because of a bunch of nuns harassing women on their way to the clinic. Forget religion! She simply could not kill the fruit of her first true love. She'd be killing a part of herself. She then called Boris to say they were about to become parents and returned home pregnant. He was already waiting for her with a bottle of champagne and some pasta tartufata – her favorite.

Sarah stretched her legs, now padded with soft flesh that had come along with the belly. She had resigned from work to focus on her exams before the baby came. When she and Boris announced their decision to both of their parents, there was a lot of cheering as if the dawn of a new age had arrived. First came love. Then marriage. Then a baby in a carriage. Sarah and Boris got married in May at the Maribor Town Hall. A simple affair with only a few guests. Her brother Gregory couldn't make it since he was stuck in the middle of an ongoing experiment in Argentina. His world revolved around ants.

What a new life in his sister's womb couldn't do, the prospect of death did. Gregory had emailed her to say he was coming today or tomorrow.

The door clicked. It must be her mother. Sarah rose from the sofa to run into her arms. She shouldn't be too harsh on her. How would she go on living without Dad?

"Hello, baby girl!"

"Dad! Hi, I was expecting Mom."

"Sorry. It's only me, baby. Can I get a kiss?"

She kissed him on both cheeks and hugged him. They stayed in each other's arms for a while.

"Good God, if you two continue like this, I'll need another pair of arms to embrace you. Are you sure you're not carrying twins, Sarah?"

She laughed. "No, only one big boy."

"Oh, how do you know it's a boy?"

"We wanted to know the gender and they told us it's a boy."

"That's great! But don't buy too much blue stuff just the same. How's Boris?"

"He's fine. Working. He wanted to come today, but he's installing a new control system in a factory. He'll join us tomorrow."

Adam shrugged his shoulders. "Well, he's young and ambitious. That's good. Was the traffic bad?"

Her father always worried about her.

"Not at all. I just needed to make a lot of stops. I had to pee at every gas station along the way."

Hesitating, he raised a hand towards her belly. "May I?"

"Go ahead. He's a part of you, too."

"Yeah, the business-minded part."

"And not the stubborn part, I hope."

He stroked her belly, detecting a punch from inside. Adam's eyes moistened with tears of happiness. "What a lively fellow you're bringing into this world. Isn't it a miracle, Sarah?"

"It is, yeah." She sighed and leaned into his shoulder. "I love you, Dad."

"I love you, too, darling."

She moved away and looked him in the eye. "How are you doing?"

He nodded to indicate he was fine and made a gesture towards the living room. "I'd like to talk to you. I really need your support, Sarah."

He brought out some cheese and crackers with juice. Sarah nibbled a bit as she waited for Dad to start.

"I've known about my cancer for some time," he said.

"But – "

"Please, just listen. This is very personal. Everyone's cancer is different. Some are curable, some are not. Mine is the worst form of pancreatic cancer. I had some pain under my ribs, so I went for a checkup. They found a big lump that has already metastasized to the liver. It was just before your wedding when they told me I have only a few months left. Of course, I sought a second opinion in Switzerland. Sadly, they confirmed the diagnosis. I didn't know how to tell you. I didn't want to spoil your happiness. Then, I didn't want to ruin the holidays. Life was still somehow normal, just a little pain here and there. Until your mom found me unconscious on the floor of the study."

Sarah took his hand, trying to control her tears. "I know. Mom told me. She was in a shock."

"Yes, I know. And I regret not telling her."

"It's not easy to face cancer. We understand."

"Thank you. So you'll also understand what I need now."

"Tell me, Dad." Sarah held her breath.

"Dignity. Control. Freedom. An end worthy of the man I am."

Control? What did he have in mind?

"Of course, you do. You'll have the best doctors treating you."

He focused his eyes on her. "I've arranged for assisted suicide in Switzerland."

"Euthanasia?" She wasn't shocked. The word "control" had already alerted her.

"Technically, it's not euthanasia since the physician only provides a lethal dose of drugs for you to take. There has to be two witnesses present – not necessarily family members, anybody will do."

After a moment of silence, Sarah asked, "What does Mom say?"

"That she will support me in every decision I take."

"Ah."

"What about you, baby girl? Are you with me?"

The sound of chatter from outside drew Sarah's attention. Somebody was at the door. At school, she would've said she was saved by the bell. She didn't know what to say.

"There's someone outside, Dad." She got up to answer the door.

"Do you understand my choice?"

"It's your life, Dad."

The bell rang.

"I need to know what you think now, Sarah."

She couldn't leave him without an answer, but she didn't have one. "Dad, I'm sorry. I need time to digest all this. Of course, I'm with you no matter what." She snuggled against him like she did when she was little and whispered, "We'll respect your wishes. We love you, Daddy."

He let her go. What did he expect? Yesterday she hadn't known anything, today he was forcing her to understand his wish to die.

Sarah opened the door before her mother could fish her key from her bag.

"Gregory called me from the railway station," her mother said, "and here they are!"

"Surprise, surprise!" Gregory rushed to hug his sister.

"They managed to switch flights and take the night train to be with us today," said Vera, stepping aside.

Behind her stood a young woman with Indian features, thick black hair, and very light blue eyes. Dark and light. She was stunner.

"Dad, Sis, this is Lucia, my fiancée. We met in Argentina." He nudged her into the living room.

"Hello, Mr. Lucca. Hello, Sarah. I'm Lucia Markič, a third-generation Slovene in Argentina," she said in bookish Slovenian.

Adam took her hand and drew her in his arms. "Welcome, Lucia. It's a pleasure to meet you."

"How are you feeling, Sarah?" Lucia asked.

Sarah nodded politely. "I'm fine, thanks. This little guy is kicking his way into the world."

Lucia's face remained serene. "I sincerely hope not. Premature babies have a lot of health issues."

"Lucia finished medicine and is now specializing in obstetrics. You can be her guinea pig for the week, Sis," Gregory said, assuming the role of a naughty little brother.

"Thanks, Bro. Your kindness is touching, but I already have a gynecologist in Maribor. Sorry, Lucia."

The Argentinian girl nodded. "I'm here if you need me, Sarah," she replied.

Her perfect oval face framed by shiny black hair remained austere, her blue eyes devoid of sparkle and emotion. Her film-star looks were contradictory to her profession. As if Madame Curie had decided to sing on stage. The Lucca family was visibly embarrassed. They still remembered Mojca, Gregory's amiable ex-girlfriend, from their last Christmas dinner. Now everything was different.

Vera went to change before heading to the kitchen while Adam entertained the young couple in the living room. Everyone was careful to avoid the subject of Adam's illness. A happy family reunion with a bitter ending. After a snack, Gregory took Lucia to Ljubljana's city center, which she had visited only once as a child.

"Did you get to talk with your dad?" Vera asked her daughter once they were alone.

Sarah swallowed the lump in her throat. "Yes, he told me about Switzerland."

"What do you think, darling?"

From the garden, Adam observed the women he loved as he enjoyed a cigar – after all, his condition couldn't get any worse than it already was. Vera had been more than a wife. A mother, a friend, a sister he never had. Sarah was his little darling.

"Dad, come inside," she said, opening the door. "You'll catch a cold."

"So what? I can die only once."

She took Adam's hand and motioned him inside. "Don't be such a baby, Dad."

He dropped the cigar in the wet grass, something he would never have done before, and sat with his family around the low table.

Sarah looked her father in the eye. "You have my support in whatever you want to do, Dad. I also want to be with you until the end. I can travel to Switzerland with you. I'm perfectly healthy," she said in a serious tone.

"In your condition?" Vera raised her eyebrows.

"Pregnancy isn't a disease."

"Do you understand my reasons?" asked Adam, ignoring their exchange.

The girl shrugged. "You wish to end your life with dignity. It's been the manly thing to do so since the ancient Roman times, hasn't it?"

Adam hugged her gratefully. He buried his face in her thick blond hair, trying to hold back his sobs, but failed. "I don't want to die, baby."

"Oh, Daddy..."

Vera joined in their hug, unable to control her tears. Minutes went by like seconds. Time was their enemy, ticking away without mercy.

Vera finally broke free. "Shall I make some coffee?"

"Yes, please," said Adam.

Sarah rewound Grieg's mesmerizing music.

Vera returned with a tray of biscuits, chocolate pralines, and steaming coffee.

"I think we might have a problem," she said in a serious tone as she poured the cups. "Gregory's new girlfriend is Catholic. I mean, seriously Catholic. If he's fallen under her influence, he'd be against your decision, Adam."

"It's none of their business, Mom," Sarah said, annoyed. "We just met her. Why would she interfere with something as private as Dad's death?"

Adam took a biscuit from the plate. "Because according to the Catholic Church, life can only be given and taken by God. Life is sacrosanct."

Sarah shook her head in defiance. "Why should we care? We're not believers."

"No," retorted Vera, "but Gregory has become one. I can tell."

"I'd have thought he would have outgrown bedtime stories by now," Sarah said with irritation.

What Vera said about Gregory's newfound religion made Adam brood. He'd arranged for the end to happen soon, right after Christmas. He didn't have much time to deal with complications. And he didn't want to pass away at odds with someone in the family. He had spared them from the daily running of his business, but after his death everything would go to them. They would have to steer the ship in the right direction. Sarah could do it, and she would once things settled down after she had the baby. He knew he could always count on Vera. But Gregory? Would he leave his research and dedicate his energy to Adam's legacy?

"I'd rather we talk about our grandson, darling." Adam pointed to Sarah's belly.

"Do we know it's a boy?" Vera asked, surprised.

"We do, Mom."

They chatted into the evening, the closing day an orange and scarlet glow in the west. A dark future without him. Adam talked to them about it, including his wish to keep the funeral within the family circle. Sarah asked practical questions about the company and his last will – things she knew her father wanted cleared out before his death. Not without a big lump in her throat and tears in her eyes. Vera listened, immersed in her own thoughts. She could not imagine tomorrow. Gradually, the velvet of night embraced the house. They sat in the dimmed light of the living room lamps and some candles on the low table. Later, they started preparing dinner for five. Gregory texted that they were on their way back.

The table was set with fine silverware and porcelain; the food was inviting. Vera ladled bright orange pumpkin soup into bowls. Adam added a teaspoon of fresh cream and a few drops of black pumpkin oil to the dish.

"Enjoy your meal," said Vera, sitting down.

Gregory and Lucia didn't pick up their spoons.

"What is it? Aren't you two hungry?" asked Sarah.

Lucia blushed as she nodded.

"Please go ahead," added Adam.

The couple still did not move.

Then, Lucia spoke. "With all respect, Mr. and Mrs. Lucca, I would like to say grace. This is a wonderful meal and I would like to thank God for it."

"I think you should thank Mom, not God," retorted Sarah harshly.

"Please, Sarah, don't be such a barbarian!" Gregory intervened.

With a nod, Adam took Lucia's hand. "Please, Lucia, say grace for us."

Everyone linked hands, forming a circle. It was different than "Enjoy your meal."

Adam felt himself transported back to fifty years ago. The nuns never allowed the boys touch their food before the prayer. His stomach rumbled as the smells of their delicious meal seemed almost to sear his nostrils. Minutes went by while one of the boys said grace for all of them. If he prayed to God, which prayer would he choose today? "I come to you today as your child, needing to hear from you and asking for your divine healing. There's so much I don't understand about life. But I do know that with one touch, one word, you can make me whole again. Please forgive me for my sins, cleanse me of all unrighteousness, and heal me from the inside out."

The Lord's will had been set for him. It was difficult for Adam to believe death as an act of love when everyone he loved would continue living after he had left. How could suffering pain be the path towards divine love?

"Father, as we sit here today preparing to eat this food, we remember Your Son. How He came here as a human being, and ate with His family and friends just like we do. Thank You for the gift of Jesus, and that we can look to Him knowing He understands our hunger. Bless us, Lord Jesus, and stir our hearts to remember You in all we do. In Jesus' Name, Amen." Lucia's voice echoed from the walls as they murmured amen in return.

Vera and Sarah exchanged a bewildered look. Was this where their family was heading?

However, it was time to break the ice and start a normal conversation.

"So, Lucia, how did you find Ljubljana after all these years?"

The girl paused in the spooning of her soup. "Amazing, Mrs. Lucca. It's incredible how everything has improved – houses renovated, monuments polished, the streets clean, churches open and lit. We had a sip of champagne at the Skyscraper. It was magical."

Adam felt compelled to speak. "I came here in the eighties to study law. Lots of parties and opportunities to hang out with friends. I found Trieste more restrictive than here. Trieste has always been very right wing, if not openly fascist."

Lucia shook her head and retorted politely, "I'm sorry, Mr. Lucca, but my relatives tell a different story. They say life was tough under Tito's cronies. Oppression, no freedom of speech and movement, no business initiatives. The Communist secret police UDBA was everywhere – spying, harassing, and incarcerating people. My uncle was imprisoned in Goli Otok, Tito's gulag, in the mid-eighties. He was released only after the fall of the Berlin Wall, his body and soul broken." Lucia's voice cracked towards the end.

Vera put a hand on her shoulder. "I'm sorry to hear this, Lucia. How terrible. How is your uncle today?"

The girl looked at her, nonplussed. "Oh, don't you know who he is? Bishop Markič."

Everyone looked embarrassed. They had not connected her last name with the famous Catholic priest.

Gregory tried to save the conversation. "Lucia, you must forgive my parents. They couldn't have imagined that you're his niece."

Everyone smiled stiffly. Vera collected the bowls. A rich meal of roast, potatoes, broccoli, and green salad followed. The mood improved a little as Adam presented a velvety red Malbec.

"In honor of our new Slovenian-Argentinian member of the

family. Lucia, welcome. They praise this wine for its aroma of blackberries, black cherries, and chocolate." He gestured towards Lucia's glass; she nodded her consent.

Sarah lifted hers. "I could use a sip too, Dad, to supplement my iron."

"Are you sure, Sarah?" Lucia looked at her sternly.

"Positive, Lucia," she retorted. Who was this girl? How dare she interfere with her pregnancy?

"A drop can't hurt. When I was expecting Gregory, I had a tiny glass of dark red Karst teran every day with lunch. For the same reason: anemia."

As if reciting from her medical textbook, Lucia said. "During pregnancy, the amount of blood in your body increases by at least twenty percent, causing mild anemia. The body must produce more iron and vitamins necessary to form hemoglobin for red blood cells. However, we treat the condition with supplements, not wine. Alcohol can damage child's brain."

Sarah looked heavenward and threw up her arms, feigning divine revelation. "Oh, that explains it all. Gregory's brain was damaged by wine during the prenatal phase. Just look at him now" – she ruffled his hair – "our idiotic, nerdy biologist who knows ants better than women."

Gregory was used to his sister's gibes. During their teens, they had fought with words and fists. He pointed to Sarah's belly. "At least I haven't doubled in size for one tiny infant. How much have you put on, fat ass? Confess!"

Vera wanted to burst into laughter – a moment of déjà-vu – but Lucia's stern face stopped her. "Come on, kids, you're not ten any more. Please behave yourselves!"

Adam gave a nonchalant laugh. "Let them fight. It's better than Netflix." he said, cheering them on. "Is that the best you can do? Come on, kids. You've been apart for a year. You can do better than that."

Everyone laughed. Even Lucia forced out a smile. Her family was obviously much more formal. She would relax eventually. Everybody in the Lucca family did.

"Do you have brothers or sisters, Lucia?" asked Vera.

"No, I'm an only child," she answered politely.

"Well, don't mind Gregory and Sarah. It's just their way of expressing sibling affection," said Adam.

After the meal, they nibbled on sweet treats in the living room. Then, Adam felt it was time to speak openly.

"We haven't touched the subject of my illness yet. Unfortunately, pancreatic cancer is terminal. You might not like my decision, but I plan to go to Switzerland for assisted suicide."

A grim silence filled with pain and loss invaded the room like thick winter fog. Beyond the windows, the night turned darker in the garden, the moon still hours away from rising and illuminating the bonsai shrubs and trees with silky silver light.

"Are you sure about this, Dad?" Gregory asked with a trembling voice.

"As sure as I can be, Son. There's no point in waiting. I want to end this while I'm still human. I want you to remember me as a strong man, not a decomposing body." Adam was adamant.

"I promised him my full support, kids. If this is what Dad wants, we must respect his wish," Vera said, putting a protective arm around Adam's shoulders.

Gregory looked at Sarah. "What do you think, Sis? Are you okay with it?"

Sarah turned her eyes towards a huge ficus near the window, its trunk was as thick as a leg. The crown, trimmed into a ball shape, showed new light green leaves. New life in the dead of the year. Her baby gave a kick as to remind her that her family was waiting for her to answer.

"I'm not sure whether this is right or wrong." She avoided eye contact with Lucia. "But I agree with Mom. The decision is Dad's. It's his life. Our only role is to support him – no more, no less."

She could see Lucia turning pale and holding her breath, but didn't care. The Argentinian will have to adjust to the family she'd met a few hours ago or go elsewhere. As far as she was concerned, the girl could take her brother – a constant source of nuisance in Sarah's life – with her. At least, Lucia had the decency to curb her religious zeal now.

Gregory went to sit next to Dad on the sofa and embraced him. "I can understand in a way, although it is somehow unnatural. Of course, there are examples of self-destructive behavior in animals, but always with good cause and reason."

"As I do, Son. I have good cause and reason to terminate my life. I'm at peace with my faith. This is the way I want to go."

Gregory sighed. "This is so sad. Why you, Dad?"

"I've been asking myself the same question. Why me? You know, it's just the way it is. Everyone has to die. The Earth is getting overpopulated. And with a new family member on the way" – he gestured towards Sarah – "the question is why not me."

Lucia stirred in her armchair. "Don't you trust the Slovenian palliative care system, Mr. Lucca?"

"Not really. I'm not so much afraid of the pain as of the indignity. Living without dignity is a special kind of suffering."

"I think Adam's fears have to do with his childhood," Vera explained, hoping to quell further opposition despite her husband's unwillingness to talk about his past, "but we shouldn't burden our first evening together with such talk."

Sarah stood up and stretched her arms.

"Where are you going?" Gregory asked.

"To the toilet, Bro. This little footballer makes me pee every half hour. Mom, we should talk about it. Dad wants it to, I think."

"She's right," Adam said. Once she left the room, he added, "I'd like you and Mom to be with me on my last days. Not Sarah though. It's not good for the child."

Lucia's face fell. She didn't dare look at Gregory, who had his head on his father's shoulder.

"I'll be with you in Switzerland, Adam," Vera said seriously.

"Dad, do you know what Pope John Paul II wrote about suffering?"

Adam shrugged. He didn't.

"It is suffering, more than anything else, which clears the way for the grace which transforms human souls."

Having returned in time to hear Gregory's words, Sarah said, "Maybe Dad doesn't need to be transformed. He's done so much good in this world while this pope of yours covered up for pedophile priests during his reign." Unable to let Catholic hypocrisy ruin her dad's peace of mind, she continued, "Bro, I don't know you anymore. Did you convert to Christianity recently?"

The awkward silence that settled in the room answered her question. Lucia spoke up.

"You must understand that life is a special grace, a valuable gift one should not take away lightly. As a doctor, it is unthinkable for me to administer a lethal drug to a patient. It is against my principles and training. I think that modern medicine offers adequate relief in situations such as yours, Mr. Lucca. Euthanasia is a very slippery slope. It opens up too many doors for abuse, like treating humans as disposable goods once they're old and sick."

Adam nodded in understanding. "Lucia, I've read about nothing else lately. Euthanasia is a controversial subject indeed. I know that in countries where it is legal, things are far from perfect – the 'mercy killing' of the mentally impaired, like children and people with Alzheimer's and dementia. I understand all this. But my situation is different. I have a terminal illness that will eventually end in pain and suffering. Why should I wait for my final breath? Isn't it my human right to do what I want with my life? Isn't this an exercise of my free will?"

His final words echoed in the room.

"Of course, we don't have to end this debate tonight. We have a few more days before you return to your lives. We'll talk more tomorrow." After a pause, he added, "Mom will be there with me, and that's all I want. To spend my last days with the love of my life."

He took Vera's hand and they drank strength and love from each other's eyes.

"I'll always be here for you, Adam."

The Last Christmas

> Through me you pass into the city of woe:
> Through me you pass into eternal pain:
> Through me among the people lost for aye.
> Justice the founder of my fabric moved:
> To rear me was the task of power divine,
> Supremest wisdom, and primeval love.
> Before me things create were none, save things
> Eternal, and eternal I endure.
> All hope abandon, ye who enter here.
>
> – Dante Alighieri, The Divine Comedy,
> translated by Henry Francis Cary

Snow whitened the plains and hills around Victoria's house, breathing silent magic into the landscape. Translucent icicles hung from the eaves like lace curtains, each unique in pattern and sparkle. Even on days when a fierce bora didn't play with the snowflakes, tossing the white slush high into the air, it was bitter cold.

Victoria's heart, however, was a lively instrument that ticked warmth into her body. New life filled her every cell and vein with fresh energy and hope. Two months after the surgery, she felt a hundred percent healed. She was confident that the results of last week's CT scan would show her in perfect health.

Her daily routine wasn't doing as well, though. Victoria was still livid with her daughter. Without telling her, Suzy had engaged a young woman to check on her every day, do the shopping, and clean and cook for her. Was Victoria her daughter's baby now? How could Suzy act as though she knew what her mother needed? Victoria had a life of her own. Among other private things, she didn't want anybody to know about her relationship with Mario. She had raised her voice, demanding to be left alone. To her surprise, her soft-spoken daughter raised hers, too.

"Mother, I can't drop whatever case I'm working on in Ljubljana and drive an hour one way every time you need something. Please understand that you need help on a daily basis. You can either accept Jana or move to Ljubljana and stay with us for the winter. Had I asked you in advance, you would have said no. So I didn't," Suzy said.

"Mario can help me. I don't want a stranger in my house," Victoria replied angrily.

Suzy was unyielding. "Mario's your friend and he can come over any time you want. But I don't think you'd like him to do your laundry or help you take a bath. Besides, Jana won't be a stranger after a few days."

Left with little choice, Victoria resigned herself to Jana's daily visits. She didn't want to admit it, but Suzy was right. Jana was a good girl in her thirties. She'd had it tough since her husband died in a car crash and left her with a young son. The money she earned was more than welcome. Still, Victoria never passed up the opportunity to complain.

Days of grey November and white December went by peacefully – mornings with Jana, afternoons with Mario. Sometimes he came early and they had lunch together. Other times he stayed late in the evening and they watched a TV show together while every so often petting Laika who lay dozing between their feet. His proposal still hung in the air, the memory as sweet as cotton candy melting on her tongue. It was a warm June evening – before her diagnosis of cancer – when he came to her house at twilight. As they sat in the yard sipping champagne, Mario drew a tiny red velvet box out of his pocket.

"Dear Victoria, it's been a lifetime, but I love you as I've always loved you for sixty years. Darling, will you marry me?"

Emotions she thought had died in her heart long ago overwhelmed her. Expectations and doubts mounted as glowworms rose into the velvet sky, luring their mates to the ultimate love dance. Yet, she could not simply say yes. Life at her age was more complicated. She told him she needed to think about it first. Then she kissed him on the mouth. He took her in his arms, caressing her skin under her tunic. She unzipped his trousers and, naked, they slowly moved to her bedroom. They made love in the moonlight as crickets sang songs of joy. Slow, contained passion after decades of yearning. Mario stayed the night. The wonder of love knows no age limit.

Then, her wicked illness had put their plans on hold.

Life was a gift. Now that she knew her time was limited, she appreciated every hour, drank its mana drop by drop.

On Christmas, she would reopen their conversation and take that next big step with her lover and friend.

Marriage is a privilege not only of the young.

She noticed Suzy's car descending the icy slope towards the house. It was workday. Why was she coming? Was something wrong with Lana? Henry? Victoria didn't care much for her son-in-law. Too focused on himself. He was not a very loving husband and often an absent father to her granddaughter. Wearing a thick cardigan, Victoria stepped into the yard.

"Hello, darling. How nice of you to come and see me," she said, embracing her daughter.

"Hi, Mother. Let's go inside. Are you alone?"

"Yes. Jana has just gone home and Mario is coming over later tonight. We're going to watch Vikings," she replied gaily. "Do you want some cabbage soup? It's still warm."

Suzy shook her head. "Not now. I'm here for another reason, Mother."

Furrows on Suzy's forehead and her formal use of "Mother" were a bad omen.

"I'm listening."

Now that she had her mother's attention, Suzy couldn't speak. A lump in her throat blocked her words. She took a folder out of her briefcase.

"I hope you're not getting divorced," Victoria said, eying the papers.

Suzy looked at her in wonder. "Why would you think that?"

Victoria shrugged. "Well, you could've done better than Henry. You're clever, pretty, educated. I never understood what you saw in him. He's selfish and spoiled. Over-coddled by his mother. Still, Lana loves her daddy. It would break her heart if you two split up."

Suzy shook her head in disbelief. "Mom, more than twenty years have passed and you still nurture a grudge against him and his mother. Leave Henry alone. He's okay."

"I'm sorry, darling. You're my only child and I love you. Neither a king nor a prince would be good enough for you." She embraced Suzy and kissed her on the cheeks.

They stood there for an awkward moment, the silence before the storm. Suzy came with bad tidings. She breathed in deeply and pointed at the folder on the table.

"These are the latest results of your CT scan, Mom."

Victoria paled. Her hands began to tremble as she realized the reason behind Suzy's visit. "It's bad, isn't it? That's why you're here."

"It's not good. Dr. Kovar called me this morning. They had the decency to ring me up before they mailed the results to you."

Victoria looked out of the window. "To where has it metastasized?"

"Your lungs and ribs. The tumors aren't big, but they're scattered and many."

A sigh of horror and disbelief escaped Victoria. Her voice trembled with resentment as she spoke.

"They said they had removed everything. Somebody obviously didn't do his job well."

Suzy went to bend over her mother and put her arms around her frail shoulders. Her cardigan was empty on the front where her right breast used to be. "The tumors weren't there three months ago, Mom. At least the scans before the surgery didn't show any."

"So, they came out after the operation."

"I am sorry."

"Instead of removing the cancer, they were sowing it."

"We should act quickly, Mom."

Victoria slipped away from her embrace. She couldn't stand being touched now, not even by her daughter.

"Why did I have to wake up from the anesthesia? I should have fallen asleep for good." Her voice broke into sobs.

The world seemed to erupt into chaos. Laika began to howl as she drew close to Victoria, leaning her furry body into hers. Suzy didn't know what to say or do. The painful news grew between them like a wall. In autumn, she had been so relieved when her mother recovered her health and was able to settle back in her village with everything she loved. Now, this new battle ahead. Would Mother find the energy to survive it?

"All's not lost, Mom. Dr. Kovar will see us tomorrow to discuss further treatment."

"What treatment? What's the point? I would die anyway."

The dog jumped up, placing her paws on Mother's shoulder. She patted Laika's head with her arthritic hands.

"We all will eventually, Mom. Don't you want to have all the information before making a decision?"

Victoria's body sagged in despair. She drew away from Laika whose tail drooped as she waited on her mistress. Tears ran down her wrinkled cheeks. Suzy took her in her arms. If only she could summon life and health back into her.

"Please, Mom. All's not lost. Let's see the doctor tomorrow and listen to what he has to say."

"I will die a hairless monster."

"No, you won't," Suzy said. "Please, Mom, despair doesn't suit you. It's not you."

"Baby, you don't know everything about me." Victoria hid her face in her hands.

Suzy thought of Mother's many pep talks when she was little. You can do it. You can be the best if you just set your mind to it. How can she administer the same medicine back to her? Maybe if she spurs her into action.

"Let's leave now, Mom. The evening forecast calls for a snowstorm. It would be difficult to drive tomorrow and our appointment is at nine in the morning."

When Victoria finally raised her face, Suzy could see all eighty years of pain in her wrinkles. Her eyes were blurred, her expression dull.

"Do you want me to pack for you, Mom?"

Victoria nodded, but didn't move.

All hope was gone. The evil was back and this time all these alien cell formations were determined to kill her.

"Will you go with me to the doctor's tomorrow, dear?"

"Of course, Mom."

Victoria murmured a thank-you. She dialed Mario and asked if he could keep the dog for two days while she went to the hospital. When he asked if anything was wrong, she lied, saying it was a routine checkup. Half an hour later, he came over and, as they said their goodbyes on the doorstep, she kissed him on the mouth in front of Suzy.

Blizzard and fog made the freeway dangerous. Thick snowflakes were falling from the evening sky and stuck to the lanes like an icy carpet. They drove slowly, wrapped in ominous silence. The only other sounds were the engine's buzz and the windshield wipers. After two hours, they parked in the underground garage of Suzy's apartment.

"I hope your husband is away. This should be our evening – the three generations of women."

Suzy helped her out of the car. "Don't worry. He won't bother us, Mom."

Lana came to meet and embraced Victoria. She gently kissed her on the cheeks. "Trust in medicine, Granny. They're coming up with new cures every day. I know what I'm talking about."

The old woman acknowledged Lana's conviction with a faint smile.

Then, Henry gave her a hug. "It will be all right, Victoria. We're all here for you."

It was perhaps the first time she had seen him as a man. Leaning all her weight into his, she felt something inside her break and began to cry.

"You're a brave woman, a winner. You never take no for an answer. Believe me, Victoria. I'm your son-in-law. I know."

They spent the evening under the gloom of next morning's medical appointment.

Victoria would never forget the lump in her throat as the doctor delivered her death sentence. She couldn't help but remember the charlatan whose words now perforated her brain like acid: "Everybody has chemo eventually."

"How long do I have if I refuse chemotherapy, Doctor?"

He looked at her seriously. "A few months maybe."

"And if I do it?"

"Definitely longer, a year or two. Maybe more. It depends on how the metastases react to the chemotherapy. Sometimes they regress to such extent that it seems almost a miracle. We must try and see. I'm sorry."

"What do you recommend, Doctor? Shall I take it?"

He slipped off his glasses and started to wipe them with a piece of tissue. At last, he looked her in the eye. "According to my training and convictions, you should. I cannot advise you to refuse treatment. Yet, you have your rights, Mrs. Jug. You can say no. Whatever you decide, we are here to help you."

Victoria digested his words. Then, she turned to Suzy. "What do you think, Suzy? Should I?"

Suzy was shocked. Whatever she answered would be wrong. Did Mother seriously want to burden her with such a decision?

"I'm sorry, Mom. You have to decide this alone. It's your life. I'm here to support you, that's all."

The old woman nodded, giving her daughter a disapproving look. Nobody wanted to take any responsibility.

When you're sick, you're on your own. Alone and forlorn.

"If I suffer too much from the side effects, I can stop treatment, can't I, Doctor?"

"We can continue or stop any time you wish, Mrs. Jug."

Victoria focused her gaze on the light from the window. It was dim, the bleak winter sun just emerging over the narrow street behind the clinic. Maybe she should trust the doctors. Maybe with their help she could fight this monster and gain more time.

"All right, let's do it. I'm ready."

They set the date of her first session after Christmas.

A week later, Victoria was sitting comfortably on the sofa, sipping tea as she waited for her family to arrive for dinner. It had started snowing in the afternoon. She knew that today her daughter was busy like every woman was before Christmas eve. Gifts, food, decorations, shopping, cleaning, cooking, wrapping gifts. In the old days, Victoria seriously wondered if she should stop celebrating such a wretched holiday. Had she been a Christian, she would go to church and worship the birth of Jesus instead of throwing herself into a cooking marathon. After a three- or four-course meal, she had a heap of dirty dishes to confront. Back then, men did nothing in the house, absolutely nothing. At least, in this regard, her son-in-law knew how to make himself useful and often filled the dishwasher.

In the twilight, the colorful lights of the Christmas tree twinkled in the windows glowing from the milky curtain of falling snow. Was it safe to drive? Were they coming? She picked up her cell phone. Suzy answered after the second beep.

"Hello, dear. Where are you?"

"Almost there. Another five minutes. How are you, Mom?"

"I'm with Laika, enjoying the silence. Jana came this morning and we prepared everything as you instructed. We even baked the hazelnut Christmas cake. Thank you, darling, thank you to all of you," Victoria said, her voice breaking into sobs, "for driving through this snowstorm to be with me on my last Christmas."

Her emotional outburst remained unanswered; their call was cut off. Before or after? She had to pull herself together. Stop being so pathetic. Tonight's celebration was meant to be joyous. Laika sprang to life, her tail waving happily.

"Thank God, you're here!" said Victoria on the doorstep. "I was worried. To hell with a white Christmas."

"Henry drove. We glided through a fairytale landscape," Suzy replied, smiling.

After hugs and kisses, they brought in bags of supplies and extra clothes.

"Who wants tea and biscuits?" asked Victoria merrily.

"Only if accompanied by a sip of brandy." Henry winked at his mother-in-law.

"Of course, my son. Come to the living room. The fire is warm."

The flames inside the potbelly stove were crackling, emitting an orange glow in the room. The Christmas tree glimmered with hundreds of lights, and the shadows cast by the sparkling balls were magical. Silver stars and garlands competed with the white blizzard outside.

"Oh, you still have Santa, Granny!" Lana touched a shiny red and silver figurine.

"Yes, it's older than your mom, Lana. Your grandfather bought it on our first Christmas together. We couldn't have a tree in our tiny apartment, but we had pine branches with this Santa."

Suzy embraced her mother. "Mom, it's so good to be here." Then, she assumed the role of commander. "Lana, place the gifts under the tree. Henry, put the groceries away." She paused. "Where's Mario?"

Victoria shook her head. "You don't have to do everything now, Suzy. Slow down. Mario is coming to dinner. We said it would be at seven."

The evening started off in a merry atmosphere with plenty of jokes. Mario was a true storyteller. After dinner, they distributed gifts. Henry brought out his guitar and they sang along as he played. Victoria would begin a song and he would continue. Lana pulled up the lyrics on her smartphone. Family karaoke from "Silent Night" to The Beatles' "Help!"

The weather cleared and the snow stopped, exposing soft white slopes to the moonlight.

"Let's go for a walk," suggested Henry.

Suzy joined him while the others remained cuddled on the sofas in the living room.

The couple marched through the thick snow, the crisp air lifting their spirits. The road was slippery. No snow blower or car had passed by for hours. Only a narrow path led to the church on the hill.

"Shall we go up to the church?" asked Suzy.

"Yeah, sure. Do you think they're celebrating the Midnight Mass?"

"Let's check. Would you like to attend?"

"Maybe."

In silence, they marched hand in hand into the Christmas evening. Suzy thought of the first years of their marriage when Lana was small and they were trying for another baby. She would buy red lingerie last after she was done with her Christmas shopping. They made love all the time, but her body felt as though it were shutting down. Lana had been conceived after years of trying. Another baby never came. She felt worthless, sad, a loser. An only child unable to conceive more than one herself. Henry comforted her, saying it was for the best since they could give all their love to Lana. Why yearn for a bigger family?

She could feel the warmth of his hand through the woolen gloves. After all these years, she still loved him. One of these days, however, she needed to have a serious talk with him. Rumors of his infidelity had reached her circles. She felt humiliated.

She wasn't enough for him. Once again she felt not good enough.

All her life, she'd tried to meet the expectations of others and her own perfectionist standards to outdo them. The best pupil in elementary and high school, top grades in law school, highest score on the bar exam. Nothing she did was good enough, though. Mother always wanted more. The pressure grew every day. Her parents enrolled her in all kinds of activities: ballet, piano, tennis, French, Girl Scouts. Her childhood schedule was busier than the prime minister's. What for? Today, apart from visiting a few classical concerts or occasionally reading a book in French, she had no need for any of those skills. All she wanted back then was to play with Vera whose free time wasn't spent on endless lessons. Despite her mother's criticism, she allowed Lana to enjoy her childhood.

Henry could feel her hand in his, too. He wanted to be always there for Suzy. Victoria. He remembered how she felt in his arms, the icy stream of despair engulfing her body and soul. Since the recurrence, she had changed. In spite of the odds, she had the will to fight. Rilke came to mind. "Only at times, the curtain of the pupils lifts, quietly…"

They had heard her crying over the phone. Crying for love. Suzy loved her mother and was determined to do everything she could for her. He understood that. He would do the same. Yet, it worried him. Sometimes you just can't win. Suzy was really putting her heart into it. She hardly slept, often working late in her office, driving to her mother, taking care of her. It was good they hired Jana – he had insisted on it. Victoria's old friend Mario could barely manage to take care of himself, let alone a difficult cancer patient.

They stopped at the little church on the hilltop. The windows glowed and the organ was playing. The Midnight Mass was at its peak and the choir was singing a carol. "Infant Holy, Infant Lowly."

"Listen. Isn't this wonderful?" Suzy said.

"Yeah. I didn't know there were so many churchgoers here. I thought they were all Communists in the Brkini Hills."

"Things change. People need spirituality and the Church knows how to lure them."

They stood embraced in the icy landscape, immersed in the singing. In front of the church, a group of men were joking and drinking brandy.

A merry tune erupted from the group: "Oh bella ciao bella ciao bella ciao ciao ciao."

It was blasphemy. And Suzy would recognize that voice anywhere. It was the song of her youth, when she ran wild over the pastures of these hills. The two weeks she spent at her uncle's without her parents. Freedom for Suzy tasted of ripe cherries high up in the tree.

"Dario?"

"Hello, Suzy." A tall man approached the couple. "May I?" He looked at Henry, who nodded in amusement.

Dario embraced Suzy and kissed her on both cheeks. He didn't let her go and they stood looking at each other's eyes, weighing years that had separated them.

Suzy finally freed herself. "This is my husband, Henry."

They chatted for a few minutes, took a sip of brandy, and continued their walk.

"He's good-looking," Henry said once they were out of earshot.

"Yes, he is. What a surprise to see him again here."

"He must've been terribly in love with you, Suzy."

She laughed. "Yeah, he was. Everybody in the village made fun of him. When he saw me arrive at my uncle's, he came to the house running. We were twelve. Always together, the best of friends. We picked mushrooms, wild strawberries and cherries, brought the cows to and from the pastures. It was fun. He was very cute as a boy, while I wasn't a pretty child. I never knew what he saw in me. You could say we were sweethearts."

Henry waited and took her hand. "He was hugging you a bit too keenly. I think he would have kissed you on the lips had you been alone. Have you two been in touch?"

Now look who's talking, thought Suzy.

"I found him on Facebook a few months ago. We've exchanged news. It's been over thirty years, Henry."

"Where does he live?"

"In Trieste. He owns a hardware factory. I'm glad he made it. He wasn't very good at school. He married into the business and has three daughters, two grandsons."

"And? Do you still have feelings for him?"

Suzy halted on the spot. "Why are you asking me all this, Henry? Are you jealous?"

"I'll understand. You're under a lot of stress lately."

"He's an old friend, that's all. My stress has more to do with the rumors about you and that translator, Tina, being intimate friends," Suzy said, her voice trembling in anger.

He stopped, perplexed. "No, we're not. Where did you get that?"

"A friend of a friend. At first, I tried to ignore the gossip, but it has reached the courtrooms in Ljubljana. People are laughing in my face, Henry. I don't know what to do."

Either he should win an Oscar or he was telling the truth. He lifted her hands to his lips. "Suzy, I swear on our daughter's life, I have nothing going on with Tina."

"Don't tempt fate with the health of Lana! I need to know the truth, Henry." When he tried to come closer, she stepped back, slipping her hands from his grip. "What's it about then? Why is everybody smirking at me?"

"I don't know, Suzy. I swear. She made a few advances, but I turned her down. I know whom I love. I would never betray you. Especially now when you have so much on your shoulders. Do you think I don't notice the long hours, sleepless nights, apathy, and depression? I try to make myself useful, but my job keeps me away most of the week. Lana and I keep in touch. It's you we're both worried about."

"It's Mother who's sick, not me," she retorted, imagining their conversations behind her back. "If Lana finds out you're screwing around, she would teach you a lesson."

"Suzy, how many times do I have to say it? I'm not having sex with anyone but you!"

"There's not much sex in your life then."

"So what?"

"Ever?"

Henry sighed deeply. "You know I've had other girls before we met."

"And after?"

"What do you want from me? You want me to kneel before you and make a vow of chastity?"

Suzy was furious. "I want to know if you've ever cheated on me. Yesterday, two years ago, ever!"

His eyes blurred. Truth. "I did."

"You what?"

"I had an affair fifteen years ago with a computer engineer working on the site in France."

"Oh, once fifteen years ago. What do you take me for? Stupid?"

He tried to move closer again, but she backed away.

"I'm telling the truth. At the time, I thought I was in love. Everything was different with her. You remember that period. We had perfunctory sex dictated by the schedule of your ovulation. It drove me crazy. To be treated like a prize bull. Then I met Nicole. But I soon realized you were the most important person in my life. So I ended the affair."

Tears sprung to her eyes. Those years were the worst in her life. After burying her hope for another baby, she had opened her law firm. Other men had never crossed her mind, though many crossed her path.

"You disgust me, Henry."

He touched her elbow. "Please forgive me. I never meant to hurt you."

"Oh, is that so? What about Tina?"

Henry shrugged his shoulders in despair. "I already told you there's nothing between us. Maybe she's frustrated. She's used to men falling all over her, so she spreads these rumors. I don't know. Who understands women?"

Suzy took a deep breath and managed to calm down. She shook her head. "What kind of woman would lie about something like that?"

"Believe me, she's the type." He moved closer and put his hands on her shoulders. "Suzy, I love you. I'm happy with you. We'll be together no matter what course your mother's cancer takes. I'm here for you. And for her."

She looked him in the eye. If only she could believe him. "At least look into this vicious rumor and put an end to it. I'm not going to stand by and be played for a fool." She stared in the distance.

He wrapped his arms around her. "I will. I promise, Suzy. Trust me," he whispered in her ear.

"I find that hard to do right now."

He wanted to kiss her, seal their love with the wax of affection, but didn't dare. She read him like an open book.

"All right, Henry Kramar. Tell this slut to shut her mouth or she's facing a lawsuit."

In reply, he kissed her cheeks softly, drying the salty tears with his lips. She put her arms around his neck and they kissed long as lovers do when making peace. On the way back to the house, the white and silver landscape filled their souls with purity.

The house was dark apart from the light in the kitchen. His face buried in his hands, Mario was sobbing, while Lana stared at the bottle of Victoria's medicine.

"What's wrong?" asked Henry.

"Where's Granny?" added Suzy.

"She's asleep. She was too tired to wait up for you," replied Lana, scanning her mother with cold eyes. "Mom, did you know the doctors prescribed morphine? Her situation is probably worse than what they told you."

Mario said, "She didn't tell me her cancer was back. We talked about our future. We wanted to – " His voice cracked.

Lana touched his elbow kindly. "They didn't tell me much either. They treat us like idiots."

"I'm sorry," stuttered Suzy. "We're just obeying Mother's wish. Total secrecy. It's her illness and she has the right to deal with it in her own way."

Suzy was annoyed by her daughter's admonition. Just because she was in her third year of medical school didn't give her the right to be judgmental.

"Mom, Dad, it's time to start telling each other the truth. Granny is going to need special care. We must think ahead and find a hospice that specializes in pain management. This is the priority. All this secrecy is bullshit."

Henry took her daughter's hand. "You're right, Lana. We should start making plans. Victoria won't be able to do it on her own."

"Mention the word 'hospice' to Mother and she'll have a heart attack."

"Have you ever asked her about it? Has she mentioned her funeral to you, Mom?"

Suzy felt trapped. "She did, but…I can't…"

Henry put an arm around her shoulders.

Mario looked at her. "It's not for children to discuss the death of their own parents with them." He wiped his face. "I'll talk to Victoria about funeral arrangements. And about the hospice, too. I'll be following in her wake soon enough, anyway. I'll see you at breakfast tomorrow. Suzy, don't cry."

She sat still wearing her coat, shaking with sobs – the only sound in the kitchen.

"Good night, Lana. Thank you for telling me the truth."

"Good night, Mario. I wish somebody loves me as much as you love Granny."

He left the house with Laika in tow.

"Wait, Laika!" Suzy grabbed her by the collar. "Where are you going?"

"Oh, let her go. We'll go for a stroll before bed."

Father, mother, and daughter sat silently around the kitchen table.

Jesus was born that night like on every Christmas eve for two thousand years while his flock continued to die every day.

Faith in resurrection is a privilege, a tale for children, and a consolation for mankind.

Real life is in the earth – growth, bloom, and decay.

Life is a tragedy without catharsis.

The Darkest Night

> So runs my dream: but what am I?
> An infant crying in the night:
> An infant crying for the light:
> And with no language but a cry.
>
> – Alfred Lord Tennyson, In Memoriam A.H.H.

Pain ripped through his body like a thousand sharp knives. For a moment, he thought he was being cut in two, disemboweled. Was there blood on his sheets? But no, the pain was within his body. His brain could not process the agony. He felt himself losing consciousness. Focus, Adam, focus. He must take his medicine now. Everything was on the nightstand. The pills, a glass of water, a cell phone for the dim light. Yet, his body was so numb he couldn't move. Just a few more seconds. The morphine was so close, yet so far away.

Finally, he moved. He gulped down a pill with some water and lay back down. The cramps seemed to ease a bit. Was it only a placebo effect? He should take the morphine drops too since it would take the pill some time to enter the sensory nerve endings. Using the cell phone's light, he counted forty drops and drank it with some water. Like thunder from the sky, the next wave of pain lashed through his spinal cord and set his brain on fire. His soul seemed to leave his body. This was the end. He was dying. No light at the end of the tunnel, no floating above his tortured body, no heaven's gate.

Just darkness in the night.

He woke up an hour later and it was as though nothing had happened. He waited for his mind to clear, then tried to move his hands, then legs, then body. All right, now it was time to get up and go to the bathroom. Slowly. In case his legs gave way beneath him.

Wrapped in a bathrobe, in the merry lights of the Christmas tree, he dragged his body to the sofa in the living room. Outside was one of the darkest nights of the year, although the calendar promised longer days from now on until June. Spring, summer, sun. He knew he would not live to see it.

Yet tonight, he was still here and alive. He breathed in the air, warmed by the beating of his heart as though his approaching end had woken his inner being to understand the miracle of life.

What was the essence of life? Was it the joy he felt in running, swimming, and making love as a healthy man in his fifties? Or was it the excruciating agony he just went through an hour ago? Christians glorified pain because it brought them closer to Jesus, who suffered on the cross for humanity. Adam abhorred pain. Before the cancer, he couldn't stand it, now he cursed it. On the news, footages from various war zones showed wounded soldiers, their ravaged bodies on display for all the world to see. That was easily avoided by switching the channel. The idea that suffering is the sublime testimony of God's presence or some other higher being is sick. It is nothing but the loss of reason and humanity. When the cancer attacked his nerves and senses, he didn't feel angels bringing him closer to God. He experienced pain ripping him apart, his primordial self at the mercy of alien powers.

The doctor had told Adam to up his intake of the pills to three times a day and the morphine to twice daily. For fear of losing his clarity of mind under the effects, he didn't do as he was told. And tonight he paid the price. He must prepare himself for more frequent bouts of pain. The progression was as inevitable as the cancer eating his body from the inside out.

Maybe he should simply gulp down all the morphine pills and drops in the cupboard. Would the overdose induce a peaceful death? The handbook for self-deliverance, which had become his bible lately, did not recommend it, as his body could have become tolerant to the elephant dosage and he'd end up waking up after a few days. Besides, where could he do it? At home? Who would find him?

He should call Dignitas tomorrow to make arrangements and set a date for him. The sooner the better. Postponing only meant having less control. He wasn't sure if he could even drive to Zürich. Certainly not with all the morphine in his system. Soon he would lose the use of his legs and he would end up either in a hospice or in a hospital where indignity would accompany the pain.

"Dad, why aren't you asleep?" Gregory mumbled on his way to the kitchen.

"Why aren't you, Son?"

Everybody was so considerate around him these days. Adam was grateful for their love, but he also felt embarrassed. He had always been the head of the family, steering them in the direction he considered correct. Now, he had lost his grip on the rudder. His family – the ship's crew – would soon be alone, lost in the stormy ocean of tomorrow.

Holding a glass of mineral water, Gregory sat on the sofa opposite him. "Would you like something to drink, Dad?"

"No, thanks."

"Are you all right?" In the colorful lights of the tree, Gregory could see the effects of Adam's battle with the enemy inside him. "Did you have a bad attack?"

Adam sighed. It was time to be honest with his son. "Yes. I took a higher dose so I might be a bit high now."

"Dad, I envy you," Gregory joked. "If I smoked a joint, I'd have to hide. At least, you're legally high."

Adam smiled. "Indeed. The world looks much better through a morphine fog. Don't junkies and cancer patients know it." Trembling with courage and angst, he said, "Gregory,

I'm calling Dignitas tomorrow. Can you drive me to Switzerland once they give me a date?"

The young man froze in horror. It had really come to this.

"I can ask Mother, if you can't. When is your thesis presentation?"

"In two weeks. I hoped…"

"I'm sorry, Son. Once it starts, the pain is unbearable. In the business world, we have a saying: Cut your losses."

Gregory understood the understatement and it hurt him. He loved his father. "I'll drive you. I can change the date of my presentation, Dad."

"Thank you."

They sat in silence. Adam couldn't help but worry. Who would run the business after he was gone? Sarah was about to have a baby; Gregory had taken a different career path and was building a life in Argentina. Lucia and Gregory's engagement was celebrated within the family circle. Her parents had come to Slovenia the week before Christmas. Simple, hard-working folks who sacrificed everything for the education of their only child. He wondered if Lucia knew to appreciate it.

"I know Mom wants to be with you. What about Sarah?"

"I don't want her there. She needs to take care of herself first. It'll be any day now."

Gregory kept forgetting about his sister's state. "Sorry, Dad. Maybe she'll pop tonight. You'll be a grandpa and I'll be an uncle tomorrow."

"That would be nice." Adam smiled. Then, he became serious, wanting to discuss the future with his son. "Let's talk about you for a moment. Have you had an offer for the postdoc position in Argentina after your thesis defense in Ljubljana?"

"I have, but I'm not sure about accepting it. Lucia and I would like to return and bring her parents to Slovenia, too. Her father is retiring in two years."

"What about their friends and community in Buenos Aires? Wouldn't they miss them?"

"They don't socialize much. They lived a very secluded life. Work, church, Lucia. They dream of an old farmhouse with fields and animals. I want to help them."

Adam couldn't help but approve. "That's very good news. Mother will need somebody to help her," he replied. "What about your research in the Amazonas? Will you abandon it?"

"Not exactly. I've done much of the fieldwork, but the project money is running out and I need to raise more funds in order to continue."

How convenient, thought Adam and felt a prick of guilt. With some training, his son would be capable of advocating the family's interests in the business. It was his dream for his children to take over. Since the diagnosis, he had also considered offers from major players to buy the company. Instead, he made Sarah and Vera primary shareholders. There was always time to sell later on.

"Had you accepted a share of the company, you wouldn't need any funding. But you turned it down last summer," he said, trying to mask the bitter remorse in his voice.

Gregory looked at him and hung his head. "I'm sorry, Dad. I didn't know you were ill."

"Yeah, I should have told you why I was handing over the business."

"I understand why you didn't. However, I've changed since I met Lucia. I want to settle down, have a family, and earn money. I'm sorry I didn't show enough respect for your work."

Father shook his head. "I never really explained it to you. Finance and ants have many similarities. Both can be intriguing." He smiled.

Gregory's face remained serious. "Until last month, since I found out you were sick, I never realized how much I missed you all, Dad – you, Mom, and even my pain-in-the-neck sister, Sarah. I want to stay close to Mom once you're gone. She'll need me." His voice uncertain, he added, "What do you think of me helping out in the company until Sarah takes over?"

Adam's heart jumped with joy. The share he had kept in

his name would have an owner. It wasn't just Gregory being considerate, it was an expression of love. He knew how much it meant to his father to keep the business within the family.

"That would be a great gift and sacrifice – thank you. I hope it won't interfere too much with your science career."

Gregory sipped some water and took his time before replying. "You know, Dad, maybe my science career, as you call it, was my way of proving myself. I wanted respect that didn't come from being your son. You know who opened my eyes? Lucia's father. He was fascinated by everything you and Mom have achieved. This wonderful house, the money, your entrepreneurial spirit that founded and built the company. He told me it was a crime not to continue your work and I should be ashamed of myself if I continue to study ants in the Amazonas while you look for strangers to manage the company. His exact words were, 'Boy, are you nuts to collect ants while your daddy needs you.'"

Adam didn't like the man's hurtful criticism of his son. "That's very rude for a future father-in-law."

"It's how he is. Blunt as a knife. Before working as a technician, he was a miner."

"What does Lucia say?"

Gregory shrugged. "Nothing really. I haven't spoken to her about this. She needs to finish her specialization in Buenos Aires. Then, she can join me in Slovenia. She should be able to find a job here. I hear they need doctors."

"It's important you speak to her. You're building a future together."

"I will, but it's weird over Skype. She'll come for my thesis defense unless…"

Adam finished his sentence for him. "Unless we have a funeral first. Don't be afraid to say it, Son. We know this is the end."

A greyish mist outside signaled a new day. In the industrial basin of Ljubljana, the fog rarely dispersed before ten or eleven. The daylight ended the darkest of nights, yet Death continued to creep around the house with his faithful prophet and companion – Cancer.

To sum up their conversation, Adam said, "Gregory, let's go to my office today and set up some formalities. You must understand how the company works. It's not rocket science, but you need to learn the know-how. I'll make you the third shareholder after Mom and Sarah." Getting up, he swayed as he tried to keep his balance. Gregory jumped to his feet to hold him. "I need some sleep now. It's been a rough night."

"Let me help you."

Adam put a hand on Gregory's shoulder. "No, thanks. I can still walk."

Gregory couldn't reply as his eyes filled with tears. He hugged Dad, feeling each rib through the thick clothes. He hadn't realized how much weight his father had lost in the last few months. Adam leaned into his son.

"Are you still sure about Switzerland, Dad?"

"Absolutely. I don't want to miss the moment."

Gregory held all of his father's weight – his fifty years, his lost childhood, his hard work, and his infinite love for Mom, Sarah, him. His Dad, his hero.

"I'm sorry I was such a prick sometimes, Dad."

"You needed to rebel to become a man."

Real men don't cry, but Gregory couldn't hold his sobs back. No language but a cry…

Under Her Skin

> I chatter, chatter, as I flow
> To join the brimming river,
> For men may come and men may go,
> But I go on for ever.
>
> – Alfred Lord Tennyson, The Brook

Snow crystals were glittering under the clear sky. The air was crisp and sharp like metal, and the cold breeze from the mountain peaks smelled of fresh linen. Vera had finished her meeting with the printer two hours earlier. Could she treat herself to a solitary walk in the glorious sunshine? Adam had company today. After a brief stay in Argentina, Gregory had wrapped up his research in South America and returned to Slovenia for good; Lucia was to follow shortly.

Like tall grey giants, the Julian Alps guarded the valley and the road meandering among farms, boarding houses, and holiday apartments. These two hours were hers, a rare opportunity to wander off and disappear. From everything. From a future as grim as the seven plagues of Egypt. From the illness that was reducing her husband into a miserable dwarf twisted by excruciating pain. From death as it crept along the walls of her home like slimy mildew. From the ceaseless remorse that she could have done something. Or done more. Angst, angst, angst – the harsh zipper in her throat.

She drove to Bled and parked the car. She would take a walk around the lake, a shining emerald set in a tiara of silver mountains. There was a bag with spare clothes in her trunk. She changed into jeans and walking shoes behind the car door. An SUV passed by, honking its horn. She gave a start. What did they see? Her breasts in a black bra? Maybe her naked legs as she pulled on her pants? Who cared? Vera was past her catcall years. These days she was invisible to men of any age no matter how fit and made up she was.

Pondering the fact that women past a certain age lose their sexual attraction, she approached the path near the waterfront. Two swans gracefully glided over the surface to meet her. The white ballet dancers with long necks and eyes turned to their fair reflection in the water. Glorious birds always in love with their beauty. Their magnificent appearance never fooled Vera. They were predators, angling for scraps of food. Ducks fled them in panic, fearing their sharp beaks.

A small boy, not more than a toddler, awkwardly approached the water. He was eating a doughnut with chocolate glaze. He tore off a piece and offered it to the swans. One of them snapped at it.

"Ow, ow, ow!" the boy screamed, dropping the doughnut.

She ran to him. The swan shrieked at her angrily; she was in the way of its prey. She shooed the birds away and looked around for the boy's parents.

"Where's your mommy?"

He pointed to the bank where a red-haired woman was passionately kissing with a man.

Vera offered her hand. "Can I take you to her?"

The boy nodded.

"Does it hurt?"

He spread his fingers and she saw the scratch wasn't deep. Still, blood smeared his peaches-and-cream baby skin. His mother, a tiny woman in her thirties, noticed them.

"Oh, darling, what is it?" she said, taking him in her arms. He leaned his head on her shoulder.

"The swan bit him," Vera said, motioning towards the lake. "Thank you."

Vera nodded and set out for the path around the lake. As though nothing had happened, the swans elegantly followed her along the waterline.

"But now they drift on the still water, Mysterious, beautiful…" Ugh. Wicked creatures adored by so many poets, worshipped by Yeats.

White evil clad in beauty.

Like her, the treacherous past clad in the rich gowns of the present.

An elegant middle-aged woman with a perfect bob, expensive clothes, and regal appearance. A black swan, an imposter.

She had started out as an ugly duckling, though. Plump, awkward, with straight brown hair and large brown eyes often swollen from crying. An unhappy child. Confused, lost, and abandoned. Not an orphan like Adam, but unloved and unnurtured just the same. Her parents were two miserable creatures with no control over their base appetites. Her father chased after skirts, mother chased after money. A little girl merely stood in their way, a good-for-nothing.

The marriage ended in a nasty divorce when she was twelve, during which she did not see her father for over two years. Although he rarely played with her, she missed him. Mother forbid all contact until the court granted Father weekly visits. By that time, they had become strangers, filling their time together with empty phrases and school reports. By the time she turned fifteen, they were so alienated that they stopped seeing each other. Mother was glad. Father regularly sent money, which was all that mattered. No Christmas or birthday gifts, no holidays. He soon remarried and she heard about having two half-brothers. She had never met them. It was too late for that now.

"Tell me about your parents?" Adam asked on their second date.

What could she say? They were nuts, irresponsible, and

cold.

"Father taught me to play chess," she said, thinking of those rare moments with no shouting in the house.

"Oh, how nice. And your mother?"

She wanted to say, She taught me to wash and dress properly, demanded excellent grades in school, and made me pay for my adolescent sins more severely than God would have done in the ninth circle of Inferno.

A teenage couple ran past her, clad in fancy sportswear. She watched the rhythmic motion of their backs – steady, brisk, determined. The girl's long chestnut hair in a ponytail brought back memories.

Vera was very serious as a teenager. She did not care much for the boys her age. In the third grade, she fell in love with her math teacher. She was seventeen; he was thirty-nine and married with two boys about her age. For the first time in her life, Vera felt truly loved and adored. He gave her small gifts, wrote verses glorifying their love, and called her my Lolita. Their love affair was clandestine, brief, and passionate. It started in May and lasted until June, the end of the school year. Holidays were compulsory family time, not meant to be spent with his Lolita. He never knew the trouble he caused her.

At first, she couldn't understand it. They had taken precautions. However, when she missed her period, she took the test. Positive. Pregnant. As she waited for her doctor's appointment, she paced inside the tiny flat where she lived with Mother like a caged puma. Restless, afraid of what the future would bring. Her plan was to finish one more year of high school, then enroll into university to study German and English. A wall of impossibilities rose before her. A baby would ruin her life. She was terrified to tell anybody. Suspecting something was wrong, Mother bored into Vera until the terrified girl confessed. How could she hide something so colossal?

"What were you thinking? You are your father's daughter! A slut and an idiot!"

Mother's angry shouts still echoed in Vera's ears to this day, although her parents had been six feet under for many years.

"Who's the father? One of your classmates?"

Vera burst into tears. She would never betray her lover, not even under torture.

"Who is it? Who?"

The girl wouldn't speak.

"It doesn't matter whose it is. We're getting rid of it," said Mother, dialing a number. "You're lucky we live in a country where a woman's right to abortion is written in the constitution."

Vera was scheduled to visit Mother's gynecologist the next day. During the night, she snuck out of bed into the hallway a few times with the idea of going to the top of the building and throwing herself into the darkness below. But an innate desire to live stopped her. She could still do it later. The sickening horror continued to loom over her that rainy summer morning when Mother accompanied her into the exam room. The doctor was a man with thick spectacles in his late fifties, red-cheeked and sweaty. She was so ashamed and desperate, she could barely greet him, much less look him in the eye.

The old doctor said, "Mrs. Leban, this is between me and your daughter. Wait outside, please."

Mother's face paled, but she obeyed.

Taking Vera's hand, he said, "Look, young lady, this happens when you make love to a boy. Let me examine you first. We will talk later."

Tears came to her eyes. The doctor understood. He'd seen it before. She took off her panties and checked the diagram above the chair that showed the correct position during examination. She lay down with her legs apart and slid her feet in the stirrups, shivering with cold and embarrassment.

The doctor came closer to her face. "Please relax, Vera. Have you visited a gynecologist before?"

She shook her head.

"It's okay. Relax. Did you use contraceptives?"

"What do you mean?"

"Did you take precautions when you slept with your boyfriend?"

"Yes, we used condoms."

He sighed. "Don't worry. I'm not here to judge you. Let's begin." His gloved fingers slipped inside her, palpating her vagina as lightly as a butterfly. "Does this hurt?"

She shook her head.

"When did you say was your last period?"

"May 20."

"It seems more advanced," he muttered to himself. "We'll take an ultrasound just to be on the safe side."

At first, she hadn't understood what he meant. Then, blood shot into her cheeks. "Do you mean it's too late for an abortion? Mother will kill me!" She burst into sobs.

He pulled out his fingers. "Easy, Vera. Nobody's going to kill anybody here."

I'm the one who'll be killing the baby, the fruit of my love. She blinked for a moment, then chased away the thought. Would he look after her and the baby if he knew? Were his confessions of love true? Or was he only taking advantage of her naivety to get to her body?

She gave a start when the doctor introduced a jellied probe into her vagina. It felt cold like death. She tried not to remember the sensation when her lover had entered her for the first time. Sweet curiosity and expectation of pain. The relief as it felt smooth and right. The heat he had inflamed. Never again. A tear ran down her cheek.

Studying the screen, the doctor said, "Vera, we have to be a hundred percent sure an abortion won't harm you. Sometimes a birth is less dangerous. But, it seems okay to me. I think you're on your ninth week."

He finished the examination, took off his gloves, and asked her to put on her clothes.

"Aren't you going to call Mother in?"

"No, this must be your decision, Vera, not your mother's." He took a blank sheet of paper and folded it down the middle.

"Here, take a moment to jot down the pros and cons of an abortion for you. Place them under plus and minus signs. Take your time," he said kindly.

For a moment, the blank page frightened her. As though the absence of reason was more dangerous than the riot of thoughts whirling in her brain. Hesitantly, she wrote School under plus. Mother, plus. Poverty, Father, place to live – all under plus. Where did her lover go? She put his initial B. under minus. She should have at least told him about this. The baby's right to be born went under minus. Conscience, minus. Health?

"Doctor, will I be able to have babies later?"

He seemed embarrassed for a moment. "I won't lie to you. Sometimes women who have an abortion aren't able to conceive afterwards. But most do."

"The ratio?"

"You've got me there. Maybe a few percent aren't able to get pregnant later."

Vera wanted to know more. "How will it be done?"

"Vacuum aspiration. It removes the fetus and placenta from the uterus."

"Will it hurt?"

"No, you'll be sedated. You will feel nothing."

She wanted to ask so many more questions, yet somehow she already knew the answers in advance. She had no choice. She had to go through with it.

A duck quacked from the lake. A male chasing its mate.

Vera quickened her pace. She shoved the memories of her younger years and the abortion trauma back into the dark. After that long sad summer, she had never spoken and rarely thought about it. Nobody knew, not even Suzy or Adam. Mother was the only cold witness of her teenage sin. Frozen Leda without her swan.

Suddenly, she heard a melody from the lake. Tourists on a boat were singing in a language she couldn't understand. Something Asian, soft and alluring. It must be about love. She stopped in wonder. "Bold lover, never, never canst thou kiss…" She wished she and Adam were the lovers on Keats's Grecian urn. To exist and never perish. To live and never die.

Although her greatest love was faced with the cruelest of all deaths.

They got married in her third year of university after Adam found a good job at an insurance company. Their two-bedroom flat was a slice of heaven. She graduated a year later in German and French, shortly followed by a degree in English. There was, however, a low demand for someone with her qualifications. Slovenia was part of Communist Yugoslavia where nepotism ruled in all areas of life. If your parents were influential party officials, all doors were open – otherwise, you learned to cope or left the country. She finally found a teaching job at a secondary school with afternoon work hours.

They couldn't care less.

The only thing that mattered to them was their love.

After the Berlin Wall collapsed in the 1990s, communism in Europe shortly followed. New forms of entrepreneurship evolved and Adam founded his private insurance company. It wasn't easy to register one back then. Old cadres in the municipal apparatus, the Office of State Transactions, which oversaw legal payments and taxes, then the bank, the premises, business permits – it was all complicated and took weeks to process. Finally, the day came when he proudly showed his certificate of registration to Vera.

Vera smiled and showed him her pregnancy test.

Their joy couldn't be greater.

Soon old fears began to haunt Vera. Something could go wrong. She took her doctor's advice seriously, ate good food, exercised, walked, and prepared everything for the baby's arrival. In the corner of her heart, the fear that God would punish her for her teenage sin dwelt like a forgotten seed ready to germinate.

In due time, a strong and healthy boy was born one May morning. They named him Luca despite everyone's comments that Luca Lucca would sound funny. Vera worried like every new mother worried. She counted his fingers, did the hearing test using two pans, was careful in placing him in the cot, took efforts to breastfeed him, and changed his diapers often. After two months, little Luca was sleeping through the night. He played with his fingers, loved long walks, and observed the world with serious focus, which would at any moment break into a wide toothless smile or acrimonious cry. At five months, he was following every move of his overjoyed parents from his baby chair.

October came with the first autumn fogs, the trees turning yellow and red.

Adam had to leave very early for a business trip to Munich that morning. Vera saw him off, checked on Luca, who was still asleep, breathing in rhythm with the beat of his little heart. She returned to her warm bed and nodded off the moment she lay down. Hours later, she woke up with a sting of guilt, wondering if she overheard Luca whimpering. It must have been past his feeding time. She quickly made a few steps to the cot.

The baby was still. She touched his cheek.

"Wake up, my little frog, it's time for breakfast."

Nothing.

She lifted his warm limp body when she realized he wasn't breathing and shook him lightly.

Nothing.

She put him back in the cot and ran to the phone. The five minutes it took for the doctor and the paramedics to arrive seemed like eternity.

Vera knew even before she made the call that he was gone. It was her penance.

She had killed a baby she didn't want.

Now her lovely prince, the cherub of her aspirations was dead.

Her guilt rematerialized.

She couldn't bear to have him taken away.

When Suzy came to the apartment hours later, she found Vera cradling the little corpse, crying soundlessly. Vera never knew how her friend found out, but she was there for her. She called the coroner, took Vera to the doctor who sedated her, brought her back home, put her to bed, arranged for a therapist the following day, contacted Adam in Munich, prepared a light soup, then waited until Adam came home in the middle of the night.

"Oh, Suzy!" He crashed in her arms.

"I'm so sorry," she replied with tear-stained eyes.

"How is she?"

"I don't know. The doctor sedated her and she's been asleep since noon."

"And before?"

"Not good. Catatonic."

"Did she say anything to you?"

"She was mumbling something about God's punishment and evil."

"Nonsense. Vera isn't religious. Did they come for Luca?"

"Yes, they took him to the mortuary. They need your consent for the autopsy. You can go there in the morning."

He collapsed on the kitchen chair. "Thank you, Suzy. You cooked." He motioned to the stove.

"Do you want some?"

"Maybe later. Did they say why?"

She shook her head.

Silence filled the space like sticky black mud. Grief was a lonely journey.

"Would you like me to keep you company for a while, Adam?"

"Yes, please."

Suzy stayed with Adam long into the night, talking about business and politics, searching for topics unrelated to the empty cot and a broken mother sedated into oblivion. They drank and cried, sobbed and whispered.

When Vera woke up the next morning, she felt Adam's back next to her in bed. She caressed his cheeks, whispering, "I'm so sorry, my love. It's all my fault."

"It's nobody's fault, Vera. Luca died. We don't know why. Let's say goodbye to him. Come, darling, we will manage."

The autopsy report said it was sudden heart failure. There was nothing anybody could have done to save him.

A week later, they lowered the tiny white coffin into a grave.

They didn't know how to go on, but they did.

Adam asked Vera to help him with the new company. It was a pretext. He feared that, left alone, she would harm herself. Behind Vera's back, he and Suzy cleaned the apartment of all baby stuff.

"Where are we going to take all this?" Suzy motioned to the heap of boxes.

"To the basement. The time will come. Maybe you'll need it, Suzy."

"Oh, I have to find the father first. I guess time will heal all wounds."

Although their grief did not go away, their love survived. They were young and busy, on their way up, on the road to success in business. Somehow the stress of everyday life dulled the memory of little Luca.

Time acted like a plough, turning over the soil and bringing new layers on the top of the old scarred earth.

Then came the night when they made love again. Slowly, one Sunday morning, like two shipwrecked souls, they sobbed into climax. It was as though a spell broke. They breathed, lived, laughed, and loved again.

Two years after Luca was taken by the angels, Vera became pregnant again.

Gregory lived, then Sarah followed. They brought her joy. Caring for them, keeping them safe at every moment was like washing away muddy guilt with fresh water from a mountain brook. Her love streamed from every pore of her being like rapids running over roots and rocks from every crack of the earth in spring.

The parents never spoke of little Luca, who was counting stars alone in his grave.

Maybe not counting. He died before he could learn to count.

Death and Pride

> Death, be no proud, though some have called thee
> Mighty and dreadful, for thou art not so...
>
> – John Donne, Holy Sonnet X

Not being behind the wheel of his Audi Q7 was a new experience for Adam, yet given the amount of morphine in his system, he was undoubtedly stoned. Besides, his body ached all over. He could barely walk and talk lately. Gregory was doing a great job driving. Adam had suggested making a stop a couple of times, but his son would just nod, turn on some light music, and drive on. Lacking the strength to insist, Father sat there like a sack of potatoes. A half-empty sack of potatoes.

After Pordenone, the fertile plains gave way to hills and woods. This winter was a mild one. Bunches of delicate white and pink hellebores, bright yellow primroses, and purple crocuses grew alongside the freeway. Forsythia bushes shone with bright yellow flowers like fragments of the sun. Adam could smell the coming of spring in the air. The plants would grow, bloom, die, then sprout again next spring. The world would continue spinning, but he wouldn't be there to witness it. In the distance, the snowy peaks of the Dolomites glittered like the bottom row of teeth on a giant shark jaw. Steep white slopes threatened the villages below with avalanches every time fresh snow covered the cracks, melting later in the year into the rivers and emerald lakes in the valleys. He was familiar with the astonishing landscape of northern Italy. How many times did he drive this road on the way to business meetings?

His thoughts turned inward, returning to memories. Business. What bullshit! The power struggle between two parties, each one keeping an ace up their sleeve. Meeting halfway was the worst idea you could ever get. There was no middle ground; there was always one side that got the deal and the other that lost and had to settle.

Like his cancer. There was only one way to win this battle: kill the cancer before it killed him.

If he could negotiate with his Creator today, which steps would he take? In business, he would study the situation and the opposing sides thoroughly. In life, this was impossible. Who could prepare for pancreatic cancer? The first step – preparation and prerequisites – had failed. Looking at problem-solving scenarios, there were very few alternatives. His main objective – life, though not at any price – was slipping through his fingers. There were no possible outcomes worth the trouble. He had hoped the Swiss doctors would overthrow the initial diagnosis, but his hope soon died. His Creator was calling all the shots. Adam was gradually losing control of everything, even his own steps.

He had never been a metaphysical person. He never reflected on his existence, where he came from, and where he was heading. His driving principle in life was to adapt to the situation without losing face. "Man is only a reed, the weakest in nature, but he is a thinking reed. There is no need for the whole universe to take up arms to crush him: a vapor, a drop of water is enough to kill him. But even if the universe were to crush him, man would still be nobler than his slayer, because he knows that he is dying and the advantage the universe has over him. The universe knows none of this." Blaise Pascal with the sharp logic of a mathematician and the profound imagery of a philosopher. Adam understood his writings, save for his blind faith in God. Adam would never follow Pascal in the realm of religion. Why would he love God and his wicked ways? What kind of man would create a human being, then let him decay in pain and suffering? Yet, in bargaining with the Creator, God was the Big Cheese, so there was no way out but to rebel and impose his own will. I will not die at God's mercy. I'll be going my own way, Adam kept telling himself the last few months. In business, he rarely backed out of a negotiation, always looking for a way to find common ground with the opposing side and help advance the business relationship towards the next deal. Every opportunity was valuable – be it a claim, a complaint, or a conflict – as long as there was communication.

"We're lucky with the weather, Dad," Gregory said, interrupting his thoughts. "Want to stop for lunch? Or do you prefer we continue on to Bolzano and have lunch there?"

"The restaurant at Hortenberg Hotel is good, but it would be nicer to stop before we reach Bolzano," replied Adam.

Gregory cast him a look. Dad was very pale, almost green in the face. This drive was a bad idea. They should have flown to Zürich. The plan to spend two days on the road for father-son bonding time imposed too much strain on a sick man.

"We're close to Belluno. Maybe we can find a restaurant there," Gregory replied.

"I know a very good place there. Terracotta or something. I'll search for it on the nav system if you don't mind eating there."

"Thanks, Dad. I could use a break, although we've already had one in Trieste."

"That was very nice, Gregory. Thank you."

"Always a pleasure, Dad. I love your place of birth."

Except Trieste wasn't where Adam was born. It was a place where he had lived until his twenties. Where the Slovenian minority was always under the threat of Fascist aggression, an ugly hangover from WWII. Everybody knew everybody – their political convictions, religious beliefs, relatives. A narrow city with limited opportunities. In the eighties, Ljubljana and Yugoslavia seemed a free and open world compared to the ageing port, a vermiform appendix of Italy. In spite of its contradictions, Adam loved Trieste. The beaches where he had learnt to swim and the villages where his foster parents, much aged by then, had taken him for Sunday lunches. They passed away shortly after he got married and his kids had no memories of them. Good people who loved him as their son. He had come late under their care.

Adam would have loved to continue along the coast to Grado and Caorle, but they were scheduled to spend the night in Bolzano before heading for Zürich in the morning.

Gregory had to keep pulling himself together. The journey did not only consist of driving seven hundred kilometers, but he also had to deal with the mental strain. He loved seeing the joy in his dad's eyes and wondered how many more times he would be able to. Dad seemed at peace sitting in the morning sun and sipping coffee. Gregory knew that Trieste was important to his father. Mother had told them his story of abandonment. All hush-hush. He and Sarah had to swear not to let Dad know they knew.

How much honesty could a family endure?

Gregory licked his lips. The chocolate taste of Illy's coffee in Piazza Unità with a view of the stormy sea and turquoise blue sky. The bora had chased away the mist and clouds, creating a clear cold morning.

In Belluno, they parked in front of the Terracotta restaurant. Without a word, Gregory guided Adam by the elbow to a window table. The father leaned heavily against his son. It was a difficult walk. He had already been gritting his teeth in pain for some time before then. Adam dissolved some morphine drops in a glass of water. His hands trembled like a leaf as he tried to drink.

You can do this, come on! He focused on his fingers to pick up the glass. This could end up disastrously. He had to be able to raise and drink from a glass without help. He gulped down the liquid in one go. Before the morphine kicked in, he always felt drained and wobbly.

"Do you need help with your pills, Dad?"

He shook his head. With some effort, he managed to fish his phone out of his breast pocket to check for missed calls. One from Switzerland. Dignitas.

"I have to return this call. Would you...?"

"Yes, of course, I'll go and stretch my legs out on the terrace. Just order a Coke for me, please."

Adam nodded and tapped the Swiss number. "Hello, this is Adam Lucca. I'm returning your call. Do you have anything new for me?"

"Yes, Mr. Lucca. My name is Ellen. I'm the secretary for Dignitas. Just a moment, please. Ah, here it is. The doctor will see you at our premises the day after tomorrow. Three p.m. Can you come at such short notice?"

"Yes, no problem. Will he prescribe the medicine?"

"Yes, Dr. Giesler will do it based on her examination and your medical records."

"I have a copy of everything with me."

"Afterwards, we just need to set the date with our colleagues in Dignitas. They'll accompany you to the premises where it will take place. They will have the medication with them. I'm sorry I cannot tell you the exact time right now. They are rather busy," she said in a sweet voice.

"It's the season for dying," murmured Adam.

"Excuse me? What did you say, Mr. Lucca?"

"Oh, nothing. What about the fact that it's less than three months from the date I initially requested? Will this be a problem?"

"I don't think so, Mr. Lucca. Your situation is very clear. I think you'll get the provisional green light two days from now. After this, it will be a matter of days."

Adam sighed. Would he be able to drink the magic potion on his own two or three days from now? He knew it was imperative. Maybe he could use a straw. The Dignitas' staff, Vera, and Gregory would be there for him, but they couldn't help him. Any physical intervention was against Swiss law.

The meal was worthy of high praise. Venetian risotto, lamb chops with grilled vegetables, and chocolate tart. But Adam could barely eat. The rice grains felt like sharp needles on his palate and the meat with vegetables tasted dry like straw. However, he drank two glasses of strong red wine while watching his son savor the food.

A grim perception loomed into his mind. Maybe there was no sense in postponing it. He should end everything today at the hotel. Why drag the family to Switzerland to be with him in his last moments? He should be leaving them with happy memories – only happy memories and nothing else.

Thanks to the wine, Adam slept the rest of the trip. They arrived two hours later at Castel Hörtenberg in Bolzano. The west glowed in the scarlet of the setting sun. Gregory saw him to his room and helped him unpack.

"I'll let you get some rest now. My room is next door. Call me if you need anything, Dad," Gregory said, heading for the door.

"Gregory, wait." Adam staggered over to embrace him. "Thank you, my boy, thank you for everything."

Such precious moments just holding each other.

"I'll see you later, Dad," Gregory said softly.

"Please put a DO NOT DISTURB sign on my door."

"Okay." He left the room.

Adam sat on the bed thinking.

What if things got delayed at Dignitas until it was too late? Should he do it here, now?

Would he have another opportunity?

His limbs were as heavy as lead. He lurched to the bathroom and took another dose of morphine drops. His third today, the maximum. He washed his face, careful not to look in the mirror. He knew the hollows on his grey cheeks, the dark circles around his eyes, and his lifeless pupils. His spirit was that of a wolf trapped in the agony plaguing his body.

"Open the cage, free your spirit, if you dare," he murmured to himself. "Prove that you still own your life."

He found the book in his bag and opened it on page 124: Self-Deliverance Using a Plastic Bag. He checked the procedure, although he already knew it by heart. He'd prepared everything weeks ahead: enough sleeping pills to sedate a horse, one plastic bag inside another for durability, two strong elastic bands, and a dust mask. He took two mini bottles of whiskey from the minibar. GLENMORANGIE HIGHLAND SINGLE MALT, AGED 14 YEARS. He planned to go under smoothly with a hint of fruity taste on his tongue. From the double bottom of his suitcase, he took out his farewell letters – each sealed with names on the front flap of the envelope: Vera, Sarah, Gregory. He sat behind the desk and scribbled a note in Italian explaining the reason for taking his own life. He attested that nobody helped him do it and asked not to be resuscitated in case he was found still breathing. It should satisfy the carabinieri.

He arranged everything on the low table and took a few steps to the window. It was twilight – the no man's land between day and night, between life and death. He opened it and listened to the birds singing goodbye to the day.

He could fall asleep to the sound of their lullaby.

He turned off the lights save for one bed lamp, sat down in the comfortable armchair, and poured the whiskey in a crystal glass. The brown and grey tones of the curtains, bed covers, and furniture were a balm to his eyes.

It was a very nice room. A very nice place to go.

How would it look in the morning light, though?

He counted the sleeping pills. Lexaurin 3 mg, 3 packages, 30 pills each.

All good things come in three.

Was he imagining it or had the birds outside stopped singing?

He took another sip of whiskey and started punching out the tiny pink pills that had more potency than a siren song. Vera had promised to bring his favorite music, "Morning" by Edvard Grieg.

There was no time for that now. He must die without music.

Would his whole life flash before him like a film?

Many who had a near-death experience claimed so.

He had promised Sarah he would call. She was due at the hospital tomorrow. Her baby was already a few days late and still seemed reluctant to leave the safety of her womb.

Adam sighed. He couldn't go without talking to his daughter first, could he?

He dialed her number.

She picked up on the second ring. "Daddy, the baby is coming. We're heading to the hospital now."

It struck him that his grandchild was on his way into this world while he was on his way out.

"How are you feeling, darling?"

"I'm fine, Dad. It's Boris who's lost his head," she said, then yelled out to her husband, "Take the red bag, Boris! The blue one is for when you pick us up from the hospital, dummy!"

"Oh, I can see you're busy. Good luck, Sarah," he said, smiling as he relived the same moment thirty years ago when he and Vera were on their way to the hospital.

"Don't hang up on me, Dad," she replied. "Tell me, how're you doing? Is Antzy Greg driving safely?"

"Yeah, he's okay. You're being too hard on him."

"Oh, I'll be even harder. I'm making him an uncle in a couple of hours. Stay tuned in, Dad. Boris will update you on the show," she said gaily.

His plan for the day fell through.

This wasn't the time to die.

"I love you, Sarah."

"I love you too, Dad. Sorry, I have to go now."

"I bet you do. Tell Boris to call Mom when he can."

"You do it, Dad. I'm sure he'll forget. Humanity is lucky it's the women who give birth or else we'd be extinct by now."

She hung up, his brave feminist daughter. Tough as a rock. She would do just fine.

His heart filled with a fleeting wish he could cuddle his grandson. Just once. Just for a minute.

He peeled off the foil from a complimentary chocolate truffle, wrapped the pink pills inside, and returned them in their package. Luckily, he hadn't popped out all of them yet. He carefully hid his self-deliverance kit back in the suitcase along with the handbook and his farewell letters. He tore apart his note to the police and flushed the pieces down the toilet.

"But I'm not tossing the whiskey away," he said aloud.

His step was lighter as he closed the window and turned on the lights.

"Let's keep going for a few more days then."

Resuming his position in the armchair, he punched his wife's number.

Death would have to wait.

Important things were on the way.

His grandson.

He smiled upon hearing Vera's agitated chatter.

Boris did call her, after all.

Last Rites Against Her Will

> "Death," said I, "what do you here
> At this Spring season of the year?"
>
> – Gerard Manley Hopkins, Spring and Death

Had she not been stuck to a hospital bed without hope of rising and living again, this would have been the best time of year. Spring, the season of burgeoning hopes and longings. Oh, would she ever go home again? She imagined tulips, daffodils, crocuses, and cherries in bloom, the air buzzing like Rimsky-Korsakov's "Flight of the Bumblebee." After the winter frosts, the fields were waking up to new life, showing off oceans of bright yellow dandelion flowers, each a universe ready to explode with seeds.

Victoria closed her eyes and sighed. Since arriving at the hospital, she had been so tired. Her vitality to fight cancer and death was gone, as were her hopes to beat the odds.

It happened two weeks ago when white patches of snow still froze during the night. She wanted to get some air early that morning and took a few steps to the end of the garden with Laika happily jumping around her. All of a sudden, her legs turned to jelly and she slipped. Her arms failed to catch her; the reaction of her body was nil. She fell facedown. Darkness. After what seemed like eternity, the dog's loud barking brought her back to consciousness. Shivering from the cold and leaning on her walking stick, she slowly got up, straightened her legs, and headed back into the house. She couldn't calm down Laika, who kept barking madly, feeling the fragility of her mistress. Warm blood trickled from her nose and mouth, salty and sweet. The sickening taste nearly turned her stomach. Yet, she had no strength to vomit. In the bathroom mirror, she saw her swollen face and two broken front teeth. The person who looked back at her was not even a remote shadow of Victoria.

She didn't call her daughter. When Jana arrived and expressed her concerns, she forbid Jana to do so either. Victoria had been through much worse than two broken teeth. Who needed teeth, anyway? The chemo had taken away her sense of taste. Everything tasted like straw. Her sense of smell was gone, too. She survived on a few spoons of soup, morsels of bread, and herbal tea. It was as though she were regressing to her childhood when she had shunned food. She didn't like meat and vegetables and absolutely hated potatoes. She loved sweets, though. Cakes, bonbons, honey. Her mother couldn't always make a dessert. It was a period of war and destitution. Now, there was an abundance of everything and she could eat anything she fancied. As soon as she mentioned pancakes, the miracle was on her plate. Everybody wanted to make her happy. She took the first bite, but the second got stuck in her throat, unpleasantly grating her soft palate, making her sick. In a second, the applesauce pancakes became the most revolting dish she had ever tried.

In the afternoon of her fall, she prepared herself against her daughter's reprimands. To something like "You should rest more, Mom," she could reply: "I'll be resting for good soon." When confronted with "You shouldn't wander alone in the yard. Wait for Jana to go with you," she'd say, "Have I lost my liberty?" And, of course, the classic "Don't you realize how sick you are?" As though she was an imbecile. "More than you can imagine, baby." When she was ready, she rang up Suzy. An hour later, they were packed to go to the hospital. Victoria didn't want to go. She didn't need a seer to know it was going to be her last trip out of her house, out of her life.

"Suzy, can we have a cup of coffee before we go?"

Her daughter read it in her eyes. Good girl, my angel. Her last coffee at home. They drank it black in silence.

"I am ready, Suzy. We can go now."

They put on their coats and turned the key of the front door.

Mario was in the yard waiting. He had come to fetch the dog and say goodbye. They held each other close for a long while. No kiss this time.

"Look what an old bat I've become. Nothing but skin and bones. Like a prisoner from Auschwitz," she said to him in tears.

"You're as beautiful as ever, my love," he replied.

"I'll call you from the hospital, darling," she whispered to his ear.

Swallowing his tears, he turned away, knowing he would not see her again.

She was his only love and she knew it.

He was not her only love and he understood it.

In the hospital, it was all about waiting. Waiting for the meals, for the doctor's visits, for Suzy to come. Always waiting. Her daily routine was comprised of long hours of staring at the ceiling. Memories were all she had. White, yellow, and orange daffodils played in the sun's rays on her nightstand. Suzy had brought them yesterday to cheer her up.

Poor girl. Nothing could cheer her mommy up.

Still, Victoria got through the day, hour by hour, using every trick up her sleeve.

Thinking of her pupils appeased her. She brought to mind their faces, names, school years, and grades.

She loved teaching history. Her pupils' eyes grew big with curiosity and eagerness when she told them about an ancient Roman festival wherein slaves became masters for one day. In every class, there would be a wiseass asking, "Can pupils become teachers for a day too, like during an exam?" Laughter and fun – she encouraged it. Young minds learned more when they were having fun. She could see them before her in rows as though at a parade. Boys and girls, fair- and dark-haired, their eyes and smiles, laughter and joy. She loved them all. Even the ones who never learned anything and never paid attention in class. She would scold them, punish them, make them study. Her love for children and teaching ran through her veins, warming her to the toes the way a river flows water into the irrigation canals in the fields. It came from her heart to every root and stalk.

Knowledge was more than power. It was the essence of life, a love for the future.

A middle-aged woman peeked in from the door of the ward. "Are you Mrs. Jug?"

"Yes." Victoria furtively checked on the patient next to her. Laura was breathing heavily. Being in the last stage of cancer, she relied a lot on the morphine, barely conscious, but a very pleasant companion when she was awake and able to speak.

Laura was a sad and lonely woman. After her teenage son died in a car accident, she and her husband couldn't cope with the loss and got divorced. Twenty years later, here she was with a malignant brain tumor. She had no visitors, save for a friend from her women's association for equality and socialist values. Victoria suspected she was a radical communist, but these days people sooner divulged their sexual orientation than their political leanings.

"Please don't talk too loud. My friend has just fallen asleep. She's in a lot of pain."

"Of course, I'm sorry," the woman whispered. "I'm Monika from the Hospice Association."

"The nurse mentioned you might come to see me. Hello."

The woman took off her elegant coat and scarf. She moved a chair closer to Victoria's bed and opened a red leather notebook. With a pen in her right hand, she looked at Victoria.

How many deceased clients were in that notebook?

She drew a line and wrote down the date and Victoria's name.

"Do you know that your daughter has submitted your application to us?"

"I do."

"So you consent to hospice care?"

Victoria was on the brink of replying something sarcastic like "Do I have a choice?" or "Who wants to end up and die in a hospice?" Instead, she raised her headrest and adjusted her pillow.

Monika was a fine woman in her forties. She wore a short blond bob, obviously dyed since her grey roots were in stark evidence. Her flamingo-colored sweater was cashmere. She'd be breaking out in a sweat soon.

"I do," replied Victoria. "It would be too much to say I'm looking forward to it, but there's no privacy here. How long can I stay at the hospice? I mean, it may take a while before…"

The woman was familiar with her concerns. A dying person often feared being sent home only to become a burden to their children and relatives.

"As long as you need to stay, Victoria. There's no time limit once you've been admitted. We've recently had a man who spent half a year with us."

Victoria winced at the use of her first name. However, she had to get used to such overfamiliarity that she would never have tolerated from strangers before.

A terminal illness stripped away an individual's basic rights and dignity.

"How are you feeling?"

Ask a stupid question and you get a stupid answer.

"Oh, like I could run a marathon, Monika." Victoria's smile died as soon as it crossed her lips.

Be nice to the woman. She's just doing her job.

"I'm not doing too well, Monika. I'm in pain most of the time and my legs hurt from cramps. Add to that the fact I can't go to the bathroom on my own."

"Don't they give you painkillers? Should I talk to the doctors?"

"They do, but the relief between doses is getting shorter. I think it's time for me to go."

Anybody else would have contradicted such a statement, try to alleviate the situation by saying there was a life ahead, not to despair. Suck it up and carry on. Monika knew better. She was a professional.

"Are you ready to go, Victoria?"

"What do you mean? I'll never be ready. I want to live and be healthy."

Monika seemed to understand. "I know and I'm on your side. I meant personal matters, though. Have you made your will and talked to your daughter about receiving last rites and your funeral?"

Victoria's eyes filled with tears. "Yes, I did. Just yesterday. I left her detailed instructions. Would you believe she took notes?" Victoria smiled at the memory. "You know, my daughter is a good girl. Very successful, too. She was the best student in school, graduated in law, and her bar exam results remain the best in all of Slovenia. She has her own law firm."

"That's amazing. Does she have a brother or a sister?"

"Who?"

"Suzy."

"Don't you have such details in your files?"

"No, she only gave her address and contact number when she filled in the application."

Victoria shook her head. "Suzy is my only child. My husband Anton and I thought it best."

Monika nodded and smiled. "I have a daughter, too. Her name is Masha."

"How old is she?" Victoria asked politely, although she had no interest in knowing.

Wasn't her dying the subject of this conversation?

"She's eighteen and studying for the baccalaureate. She wants to go to the medical school."

"Like my granddaughter. It's hard to get in and even harder to study."

Victoria thought of Lana who'd researched everything about breast cancer and reported her findings. She never embellished the situation, just told her granny the possible outcomes. Victoria was grateful for the truth. Lana was like her. Direct, no nonsense. Oh, how she would like to see her thrive. Maybe she would find a boyfriend and start a family. Little great grandchildren who would climb cherry trees and catch tadpoles in the stream. Bitter brown sadness came over her.

"What's wrong, Victoria?" Monika asked, noticing the change in her mood.

She paused, uncertain. Was this woman the right person to talk to about this? "Monika, can you do me a favor?"

"Yes, of course."

"I'm a bit scared, but not afraid to die. However, there is one thing I do know: I don't want any of my loved ones around me when the time comes."

Monika raised her eyebrows. "Oh, it's usually the opposite. People don't want to die alone."

Victoria sighed. "I'm sorry. I'm not like other people."

"You're a fighter."

"More like a coward, maybe. I don't think I can pass on if I see my daughter's angel face hovering over me."

"All right. How may I help you?"

"Please explain to my daughter and her family that I love them too much to let them go. I won't be able to die in peace if they're around. Does that make sense?"

Monika nodded. "It does, Victoria. I'll talk to Suzy. Anyway, I think you still have life in you." She touched her hand.

Victoria squeezed it, strangely grateful to this stranger for being there. "Good. Thank you."

"What about receiving last rites?"

"What do you mean? A priest?"

"Yes. We can ask for one if you like."

Victoria's voice turned to ice. "Thank you, Monika, but no. I lost my faith when I was twelve and with good reason, too. I don't want any priest near my bed at any time, dead or alive."

"I understand. You can always change your mind."

"I won't change my mind," Victoria said in a shrill voice. She lowered her headrest and closed her eyes, signaling their chat was now over.

Monika took her things and silently left the ward.

Victoria thought back to the last few months as she struggled with the nasty disease. She'd tried her best to fight it, but her best wasn't good enough. The fall took its toll no matter how faithfully she followed the doctor's instructions. When the chemotherapy weakened her heart, she allowed them to insert a pacemaker. It stabilized her heartbeat, but her overall healthy continued to decline. She had already lost her appetite some time ago and knew it was a sign that death was close. Still, she hadn't wanted to give up. Life was inviolable. An inexplicable will to survive fueled her body. Sometimes she felt how her mother must have felt during WWII when she opposed the Fascists and the Nazis by nursing wounded partisans before their very eyes. Stubborn as a rock, Victoria persisted and persisted. A gust of spring air from the window was enough to make her cherish another moment of existence. Her desire to live went beyond reason. She hung to every second no matter the price.

She dozed off for a moment, immersed in the images of her homeland in bloom.

"Let us pray together, Laura. O Lord God of goodness, and Father of mercies, I draw nigh to Thee with a contrite and humble heart; to Thee I recommend the last hour of my life, and that judgment which awaits me afterwards."

Victoria sat up in bed. She could see the back of a man in a grey tweed suit with a white collar. A priest.

Had Laura asked for the priest in her last moments of life?

"Hello, sir," she greeted politely.

The priest – a small man with large full-rimmed glasses,

thinning grey hair, and a determined look in his blue eyes – turned to her. "Hello, sister. Let us pray for Laura's soul together."

She shook her head. "I don't think Laura wants prayers in her last hour. I've been here with her for two weeks and she told me she wasn't a believer."

The man nodded, then continued his litany as though Victoria hadn't said anything. "Merciful Jesus, have mercy on me. When my feet, benumbed with death, shall admonish me that my course in this life is drawing to an end, Merciful Jesus, have mercy on me."

Victoria was confused. Dying was sacred. A transcendental passage. She shouldn't interfere.

But this was wrong. She knew Laura couldn't have asked for a priest. At least not during their time together in the ward.

"Father, I'm sorry to interrupt, but I think you've got the wrong bed. Somebody else must have asked for you and you're keeping that person waiting. Let me call the nurse." Victoria pressed the red button.

The priest stopped his prayer and looked at her with rage in his face. "Madame, you have no right to disturb the last rites of this sick woman. Who are you to stand in the way of her salvation? Our prayers will bring her to God." He took Victoria's hands and joined them in prayer. "You should instead pray with me for her soul".

"When my hands, cold and trembling, shall no longer be able to clasp the crucifix, and shall let it fall against my will on my bed of suffering, Merciful Jesus, have mercy on me."

"How dare you touch my hands, Father!"

Laura jerked in her bed. Victoria screamed like a little girl. Seventy years ago, a priest had joined her hands in prayer, too. She remembered kneeling at a pew and reciting litanies when a pair of filthy fingers suddenly grabbed her buttocks and slid between her legs. Her body never forgot the horrid sensation of that touch and left a crimson stain on her soul forever. Back then, she managed to escape. She ran from the priest, the church, and Lord Jesus as fast as she could. In reprisal, he banished her from church and did not allow her to receive confirmation. She was the only child in the village who wasn't confirmed.

"I beg your pardon, madam! Is your heart made of stone? Pray with me for your poor friend, Laura!"

Victoria hated feeling impotence. She couldn't even get up and put an end to the unwanted ceremony.

"When my eyes, dim with trouble at the approach of death, shall fix themselves on Thee my last and only support, Merciful Jesus, have mercy on me. When my ups, cold and trembling, pronounce for the last time Thy adorable Name, Merciful Jesus, have mercy on me."

Laura moved her head and opened her eyes wide. "No, no, no, please, no!" she moaned.

The priest continued as though she were not there. "When my face, pale and livid, shall inspire the beholders with pity and dismay; when my hair, bathed in the sweat of death, and stiffening on my head, shall forebode my approaching end, Merciful Jesus, have mercy on me. When my ears, shall to be forever shut to the discourse of men, shall be open to that irrevocable decree, which is to fix my doom for all eternity, Merciful Jesus, have mercy on me."

Victoria's rebellious mind spoke. "Jesus certainly can't have the mercy on the likes of you! Imposter! You weren't called to this deathbed! Go away!"

He paused for only a moment. Seeing that Laura – the object of his fervent faith – had closed her eyes in pain, he said, "I'm here to save her soul! Let me do my job, woman! When my imagination, agitated by dreadful spectres, shall be sunk in an abyss of anguish; when my soul, affrighted by the sight of my iniquities and the terrors of Thy judgments, shall have to fight against the angel of darkness..."

"No, no, please, no..." Laura's groans grew louder.

"Stop! You're the devil! Can't you see she doesn't want your prayers? Go away! Score points elsewhere!"

"…who will endeavor to conceal from my eyes Thy mercies and to plunge me into despair, Merciful Jesus, have mercy on me."

The door opened and the head nurse entered. She exchanged a knowing look with the priest, then came to Victoria's bed.

"What is it Mrs. Jug? Are you in pain?"

Next to her, Laura murmured, "No, no, no, please…"

"Nurse Nina, please ask the father to leave Laura's bed. She obviously doesn't want to receive the last rites and ointment. She's not Catholic."

The nurse looked at Victoria in shock. "Victoria, people say all kinds of things in their last moments. Laura asked for a priest. That's why we called Father Benjamin to her bed. I'm afraid her time has come." She spoke slowly in a very sweet voice.

Victoria wasn't easily put off. "This is a mistake. Please ask Father Benjamin to leave her alone. Let her die in peace. I'm sure Laura isn't Catholic. He shouldn't do what he's doing. It's like…It's like rape!"

"Dear Jesus!" exclaimed the nurse.

The priest continued. Victoria's words had no weight in the realm of the holy.

"When my poor heart, oppressed with suffering and exhausted by its continual struggles with the enemies of its salvation, shall feel the pangs of death, Merciful Jesus, have mercy on me."

"No, no, no…" Laura's moans became strained.

Victoria fell on her pillows. She was exhausted. Why was the world so full of evil? She began to sob.

Nurse Nina leaned close to her. "What is it, Victoria? Do you want me to transfer you to another room while Laura is saying goodbye to this world?"

"You don't understand, Nina. Laura is not Catholic. Please check your notes again. Call somebody close to her. There's that friend of hers. I'm sure she hasn't asked for last rites. Just listen to her moaning," Victoria said now in pain.

"There's nobody I can call for Laura. She has no living relative, Victoria."

"She's got me. I'm here. I can hold her hand and comfort her. Please listen to me."

The nurse shook her head.

Victoria's plea was as thin as the weakest reed in a storm.

"Are you hurting, Victoria?"

"I am. Please give me something. I don't know whether it's my cancer or witnessing this." She motioned to the priest's back. "It's spiritual rape. How can you let this happen, Nina?" she whispered with her last strength.

"When the last tear, the forerunner of my dissolution, shall drop from my eyes, receive it as a sacrifice of expiation for my sins; grant that I may expire the victim of penance; and then in that dreadful moment, Merciful Jesus, have mercy on me."

Nurse Nina's face was full of compassion as fake as love purchased from a prostitute. "Of course, Victoria. I'll get you something for the pain. Let me go find the doctor."

All energy evaporated from her mind and body. She was an empty vessel burning on a stove, the pain inside her torturing like fire as she waited for the morphine injection to alleviate it. She felt the warmth of urine in her diaper. In a few minutes, the stench of her decaying body would reach her nostrils.

"When my friends and relations, encircling my bed, shall be moved with compassion for me, and invoke Thy clemency in my behalf, Merciful Jesus, have mercy on me. When I shall have lost the use of my senses, when the world shall have vanished from my sight, when my agonizing soul shall feel the sorrows of death, Merciful Jesus, have mercy on me. When my last sighs shall force my soul to issue from my body, accept them as the children of a loving impatience to come to Thee. Merciful Jesus, have mercy on me."

Waiting. Waiting. Waiting for the morphine, the minutes like hours. She gritted her teeth so as not to cry out loudly.

Outside, the day was ending, the scarlet sky daubed with white clouds like an obedient flock of sheep. Heaven couldn't be more beautiful.

"No, no, no…" mumbled Laura almost inaudibly.

"When my soul, trembling on my lips, shall bid adieu to the world, and leave my body lifeless, pale, and cold, receive this separation as a homage which I willingly pay to Thy Divine Majesty, and in that last moment of my mortal life, Merciful Jesus, have mercy on me. When at length my soul, admitted to Thy presence, shall first behold the splendor of Thy Majesty, reject me not, but receive me into Thy bosom, where I may forever sing Thy praises, and in that moment when eternity shall begin to me, Merciful Jesus, have mercy on me."

Not another unwanted prayer, please. I must ask Suzy to take me away from here tomorrow. The pain started somewhere in the lungs and spread down the spinal cord to every fiber of her wretched body. What was taking the nurse so long?

Then, she could no longer be silent. "Ow, ow, owwww!" she howled.

"At last, my daughter, at last you see the divine light. Pain brings you closer to God, sister. Let us pray. O God, who hast doomed all men to die, and hast concealed from all the hour of their death, grant that I may pass my days in the practice of holiness and justice, and that I may be made worthy to quit this world in the peace of a good conscience, and in the embrace of Thy love, through Christ our Lord. Amen."

Victoria passed out long before Amen.

Father Benjamin held Laura's hand until her last breath, murmuring prayers in a soft voice. His belligerent tone was subdued by his sincere wish to ease the woman's passage to a better world. She sighed one last time. He crossed her forehead and wiped the tears from her face with a soft cotton cloth. You resisted joining our Lord Christ in Heaven, sister, now rest in peace. He caressed her cheeks, then drew the sheet to cover her head. He looked at Victoria, wondering if she was telling the truth. Was Laura a Catholic or not? It seemed strange how scared she was of God's Word. Terrified as though burning in Hell. Yet, Father Benjamin was used to resistance.

True faith was rare these days, although it was the only thing that gave meaning to life and death.

He closed his Bible and took a tiny notebook out of his breast pocket. Furtively, he scribbled a few notes to himself. A habit he acquired lately in his less and less popular profession. Although he remained obstinate in his pursuit of truth. Like a rock, like Peter. For you were like sheep going astray, but now you have returned to the Shepherd and Overseer of your souls.

The Bishop had been pleased with his work. In his last moments on earth, he managed to bring many a lost sheep back on the path to God.

"Driven by the forces of love, the fragments of the world seek each other so that the world may come to being," wrote Pierre Teilhard de Chardin, his favorite philosopher.

"Have they both passed?" asked Nurse Nina, peeking in from the door.

"No, only Ms. Laura. Victoria is in terrible pain, I think. She has lost consciousness," he replied.

"We're here to give her more morphine. We don't want her to suffer."

The nurse opened the door with a young doctor in tow. They examined Victoria's pulse and breathing before adjusting the injection into her IV.

"I guess this is it, Sister Nina. I'll be going now," said Father Benjamin.

"Thank you. I'll call you next time we need you."

"Yes, any time, day or night. It's never too late to embrace our Lord Jesus Christ and find salvation."

Be near me when my light is low

> Be near me when I fade away,
> To point the term of human strife,
> And on the low dark verge of life
> The twilight of eternal day.
>
> – Alfred Lord Tennyson, In Memoriam A.H.H.

Lightning split the sky. Clashing clouds submerged the landscape under a torrent of rain. According to the forecast, cold winds would turn the rain into snow as the day progressed. A winter tale without him. The road towards the industrial outskirt of Zürich was empty. The car ran smoothly through nature's fury, the engine humming with the squeaking wipers that cleared the rain as soon as they fell on the windshield.

You can't expect anything less from a Mercedes, thought Adam. He was seated in the front next to their driver. In the back, Vera gave a start as thunder struck the earth and roared like an angry god. Thor had dropped his hammer. Gregory took her hand and gave it a light squeeze. They exchanged an anxious look.

It was a good stormy morning with the adventure of dying ahead of him.

He must make space – only two days ago a little Adam had cried his way into the world.

Sarah had sent him the picture of a healthy boy named after Adam. A tiny baby with a wrinkled face buried under a soft blanket would take the baton and conduct the orchestra of life once he was gone. He counted his blessings. He managed to live to be a grandfather. There was nothing better to take with him to the Dignitas clinic than the gift of this new life, a wonderful concerto of emotions, aspirations, and prospects for the future. Adam's music was slowly fading and it was a good thing. No more pain, no more anxiety, only eternal sleep. He didn't know if there was anything after death, but he would find out soon. He did not abandon hope for a happy journey. His life was full of surprises and he always managed to look ahead with optimism.

"How's my granny back there?" he asked cheerfully.

"Good," Vera said in a clipped tone.

"Oh, I bet you're still struggling to take it in. Yesterday a mother, today a grandmother." He half-turned and reached out to touch her knee. He could see she was crying.

What was he supposed to do? His end was coming one way or the other.

"Son, Vera, thank you for coming with me today," he said, trying to keep his voice from breaking.

The driver, an olive-skinned Indian in his sixties, cast him a look. He knew where he was taking their family. He had joined Dignitas as a volunteer after seeing off his wife. An escape from the agony of a deadly cancer.

Adam couldn't stand the grim silence. He had to keep everyone's spirits up.

"Where do you come from, sir?" he asked politely in German.

"My family is from Bombay, India." The driver smiled.

"Were you born in Switzerland? Your German is impeccable."

"No, I came with my parents when I was five. My father was an engineer for ASEA Brown Boveri. He sent me to the university – ETH, of course. I ended up as a professor in electrical engineering there. I retired a few years ago," he said, giving a brief outline of his life story, most certainly not for the first time.

"How admirable. I thought you were a doctor or a hospice worker of some kind. What brought you to Dignitas?"

The white-haired Indian with the noble features of a Buddha statue kept his gaze on the road. "My wife. She had cancer and was in terrible pain. As a human rights lawyer, she believed in Article 8 of the European Convention on Human Rights."

Adam had naturally studied discussions on MAS, PAS, and euthanasia. In Slovenia, the public opinion sided with the Catholic Church. In accordance with the Declaration of Geneva, all doctors were made to swear to "maintain the utmost respect for human life." Even if that meant ignoring quality of life and inflicting nothing but pain and humiliation on the patient. A nursing home physician was only recently charged with several murders for administering fatal sedatives to elderly patients suffering from all kinds of ailments.

Since the beginning of his illness, Adam knew he had to take things in his own hands. Slovenia was a country where principles were more important than people. Why did he have to flee and seek help in a foreign country like an immigrant? When would his homeland adopt the fundamental humane concepts of a civilized society?

"We're here." Their driver steered the car into a parking lot.

The charming blue bungalow seemed completely out of place next to the high wall of an industrial building.

"Is this it?" Adam asked.

"Yes."

"I didn't expect this. I imagined a house in a village or in the historic center of a town. Something more atmospheric," he murmured.

"It's not legally possible for a location in the city center, only in the industrial zone."

"Out of sight, out of mind, eh?"

Why was death such a stigma? Was it because people couldn't face their mortality? They viewed the process of ageing – so natural to animals and plants – as a catastrophe. Death was unimaginable. But even if the universe were to crush him, man would still be nobler than his slayer, because he knows that he is dying and the advantage the universe has over him. The universe knows none of this.

Saddened, Adam held his head up in pride. The cancer might have crushed him, but deep down he felt as brave as a tiger.

Death wasn't easy. He'd be the last to display any weakness now.

The driver rang the bell as though they were there for a social visit. The door opened. A smiling grey-haired woman welcomed them. Adam wondered if she was the one who would present him with the lethal medicine in his last moments. They stepped inside.

Hello death, goodbye life.

Adam entered. The living room was like any other living room in the world, save for a hospital bed with clean colorful linen in the corner. It was a lovely two-bedroom house with large windows and a wonderfully kept garden. Gregory and Vera followed in tow.

"Would you like a cup of coffee or tea, Mr. Lucca?" the driver offered.

He looked at Vera, who nodded. She couldn't let him go just like that. The driver headed towards the kitchen.

"This is a nice house," Gregory stammered, leading his mother to the sofa.

"Well, it should be. This is a very important day in your father's life, Gregory."

The young man startled when she spoke his name. The Dignitas staff knew all about their family. The woman realized her mistake.

"I'm sorry. I know Nadeem has told you about himself in the car. I'm Angela Ross, a retired French teacher and a volunteer. We'll be accompanying you today. Your names are all in the file with everything your father told us about you."

"So you know I'm Vera and this is our son, Gregory. Our

daughter Sarah won't be with us as she has just given birth to our first grandson."

Angela's face lit up with joy. "Oh, how wonderful. Congratulations to all of you!"

Adam sat down in a comfortable armchair. "Yeah, I'm a lucky man. I wasn't sure if I'd live the day. As I understand, Ms. Ross, you have to talk to me about today's procedure."

Vera touched his hand. "Let's have coffee first, darling. By the way, Ms. Ross, I brought some music. Can we put it on?" She took the CDs out of her bag and handed them over.

"Yes, of course. Call me Angela, please. Which one shall I put on first?"

"The Chopin concerto, please," answered Adam.

He knew the procedure by heart. He had watched numerous films on assisted suicides at Dignitas: The Suicide Tourist, Terry Pratchett's, and others. Yesterday Dr. Giesler examined him. Then, they talked about the pain in spite of the higher morphine injections he'd needed in the past week. She said he looked better than his medical records showed. The attractive young doctor couldn't imagine how much effort it took for him to talk to her. After an hour, she gave him the green light. They had a very good and useful discussion. She told him that the medicine was very bitter and sometimes caused vomiting. Therefore, they would give him something for his stomach half an hour before. He must drink the lethal dose in one go – not sip it – then quickly follow it up with a sweet juice. Within ten to fifteen minutes, he would stop breathing and death would set in. She reminded him a few times that he could always change his mind and put a stop to everything. It was his decision as to when and how to end his life.

While the coffee brewed down the hall, Angela took out the paperwork and went through the procedure with Adam one more time. He signed several documents, namely a Voluntary Death Declaration and his agreement to being filmed so the Swiss authorities could declare suicide and exclude anyone's intervention in it. Nadeem brought him the medicine for his stomach.

"Adam, you understand why we have to film it, don't you?" Angela asked him cautiously.

"I do, thank you," he replied, relieved when the formalities were finally over.

The last few months had been a race against time and pain.

How could a man exist in war with his body?

Like that tale about being chased by a tiger to the edge of a cliff and leaping to one's death on the rocks below. His tiger was the draconian pain that medication could no longer keep in check; the cliff was the decision to end of his own life while he still had the power to do so. He embraced the idea of crashing onto wild waves and rocks similar to those at the famous La Jument lighthouse in Brittany. Ten-meter waves that roared against the rocks a hundred feet below. Such power! Such determination!

Precisely the strength he needed to set him on his way.

Looking back, he had never been afraid to step outside his comfort zone. Maybe it was due to his childhood, maybe it was in his nature. He'd always taken the rocky path instead of the easy way. There were times when he wanted to blend in and just be a piece of the humanity puzzle – nothing more, nothing less. Yet his desire to find happiness and meaning and his love for life were his alone. They couldn't be experienced as a collective, only as an individual. The only people he could ever share his moments of joy with were his family. In their loving arms, he felt safe. How would they remember their last day together? Was he being egoistic?

"Vera, Gregory, I hope you don't resent me for bringing you here," he said when Angela left to fetch the coffee and cakes from the kitchen.

Vera stood up and kissed him on the lips. "Don't forget I'll always love you, my Romeo," she whispered.

In response, he recited with pathos:

"…and, when he shall die, Take him and cut him

out in little stars, And he will make the face of heaven so fine That all the world will be in love with night And pay no worship to the garish sun."

"You never cease to amaze me, Adam."

"I love some parts from Romeo and Juliet so much I know them by heart. They remind me of us, Vera. Except we got to live to see our children grow up and our grandson born. Aren't we a lucky pair of star-crossed lovers?"

Gregory watched his parents with tears in his eyes. He rose and hugged his dad from behind. "Sarah and I couldn't want for a better father. Thank you, Dad."

Nadeem and Angela returned with two trays. Everyone sipped coffee while Angela went through the procedure with Adam once again. He was tired to being asked if he had changed his mind. At last, Nadeem brought in two glasses – the lethal dose and the apple juice.

Grieg's "Morning" filled the room with glory. The flutes overrode the sounds of the storm and thunder outside and brought Adam comfort.

He nodded to Angela. "It's time."

"Would you prefer to lie on the bed?"

Adam shook his head. "No, I'll sit on the sofa with my wife and my son by my side."

Nadeem offered him a hand and helped him to the sofa. Adam felt weak on his legs. Were they giving out now? Or was his body being paralyzed by angst, knowing these were his last steps?

Nadeem set up the video camera and turned it on.

Holding up the glass filled with clear liquid, Angela asked him for the last time, "Adam Lucca, are you certain you want to drink this medicine even though it will put you to sleep and cause your death?"

"Yes, I am sure."

Why does she keep asking? I'm not planning to die several times. One death is enough for me, Adam thought as he lifted the glass.

"Cheers!" He managed to smile before gulping it down. First the poison, then the juice.

Afterwards, Adam hugged Vera and Gregory and held them close to him.

"Happy journey, darling."

"I love you, Dad."

"Be strong, darling."

"I will."

"Gregory, keep your Mom busy with another grandchild."

"Dad, I will. And I promise to be the best uncle to little Adam."

"Yeah, say hello to Sarah for me. Tell her, everything went well."

"We will, my love."

Angela moved closer, a paper napkin in her hand.

With one last look, he took in the room, the white curtains of snow falling outside, and all the people with him.

"Thank you to all of you. I had a great life…" He closed his eyes, his body slowly shutting down.

The flutes came to a crescendo in the silence after his last words like merry bird songs in spring, like eternal creek running over rapids, like an outpouring of joy for all the life that would go on.

Adam Lucca moaned and shivered, then fell into a deep sleep. By the time the violins picked up the morning theme, he was gone.

They sat in his final embrace for a few minutes before letting go.

"I can't believe how rational and smooth it was," said Gregory, surprised.

His mother nodded absent-mindedly. Caressing Adam's still cheek, she said, "You left us with many happy memories. We will miss you, my love."

Angela and Nadeem waited discretely until the music died. After death, silence was a balm.

Finally, Angela said, "We must call the authorities now, Mrs. Lucca."

"We understand," replied Gregory.

Outside, the snow was falling in big thick flakes. Winter covered the industrial zone in white magic without any of the workers in nearby factories noticing.

Frost shackled their hearts.

Vera fell into Gregory's arms and burst into sobs. He held her tight, patting her back and caressing her hair, trying to stay calm and be a man.

The unthinkable was behind them. Only last night they'd gone out for dinner, choosing the most exquisite dishes and champagne from the menu. They talked and laughed as though celebrating an anniversary. His dad took enough morphine to get him through the evening. There was nothing somber in the air – no thought of death or the emptiness beyond it. At one point, they called Sarah on Skype and talked to her. Not for long, though, since the baby started to cry. Demanding little fella. Before leaving the restaurant, Mom and Dad even danced a bit to the waltz playing in the background. The serious Swiss diners took them for lunatics.

His father had lived and died as a hero.

"Would you like to have a copy of the footage?" asked Nadeem.

Vera shook her head, but Gregory nodded.

"Yes, please. Can you send it via email?"

"Why Gregory?"

"For Sarah, Mom."

She nodded and went to the window. The bench in the garden was empty save for the snow covering the wood and metal in white lace.

The future was uncertain, lonely, and strange.

Her life after Adam would be cold and empty like that bench.

Crows on the Roof

> Crows assemble in the bare elm above our house.
> Restless, staring: like souls
> who want back in life.
>
> – Jenny George, Migration

The park around the psychiatric hospital was empty, all the benches under the shady horse-chestnut trees unoccupied. In May, the sweet scent of the white and yellow flower panicles buzzing with bees and bumblebees was evocative. Love was in the air.

That morning, however, Henry couldn't rejoice with the spring life around him. Heartbroken, he sat on a bench with a bouquet of red roses beside him. Twenty-six half-opened buds on long stems, one for every year he and Suzy had been together. He knew it would make her happy if only for one moment. In the face of her mental breakdown, he felt impotent and weak.

When Lana found her mother catatonic in Victoria's apartment where she sat on the floor among old photo albums, she knew what she had to do: call for an ambulance.

Ever since the funeral, Suzy had started falling apart week after week. If only they had paid more attention. Her neglected clients were calling their home just to talk to their lawyer. Her insomnia, the late movies, too much food and alcohol. First, the half-empty bottles of whiskey, cognac, and brandy; then the liquor cabinet empty, the bottles in the trash. In the morning, pots of coffee, no breakfast, no makeup, her greasy hair in a bun. Henry found out later that her office was in shambles. She would go in only to postpone court hearings and distribute her clients and cases among her colleagues. Apart from drinking, Suzy spent hours on the internet. Her secretary was devastated since they were losing clients by the hour. After work, Suzy would lunch at a nearby fastfood joint and spend the rest of the day at Victoria's apartment, putting her things away and preparing the place for sale or rental later. Lana could sense something was wrong with her mother. However, her exams and study assignments consumed all her energy. They had thought that after the funeral, their family crisis was finally over. How wrong they were.

Being the perfect daughter, Suzy organized the funeral according to Mother's wishes. Her obituary in the daily paper included verses from her favorite women poets. With Vera's help, she wrote a wonderful eulogy and hired a professional actor to read it. As long as there is one person who remembers my name, I am not dead. The ending left no eye dry. She carefully chose the music – a female solo of "Ave Maria", a male voice choir singing a few of her favorite folk songs, and a trumpet solo of "Il Silenzio" while her urn was lowered into the grave. Flower arrangements in white and yellow, simple but elegant. A service with only a circle of close family and friends invited. Then, as dictated by custom, a reception at a nearby restaurant where they shared memories.

Mario was there, too. He brought Suzy a large basket filled with honey, walnuts, and various dried fruits. He held her in his arms for a long time.

"I have nobody now. Please come to visit sometimes. Laika misses you."

She promised she would. Yet, two months later, she still hadn't returned to the village or planted new crops in the fields. Mario called her on the phone a few times to tell her about the garden and the house. She always apologized, saying she was still catching up on work that had piled up during the time she was taking care of Mother. After a few calls, he gave up.

She spent most of her weekends in Victoria's apartment, reading old letters, arranging books, and selecting photos.

As she mourned, Suzy built a wall around her.

She avoided her clients, friends, and family.

In her heart, she avoided life.

Henry spent the sunny weekends biking fifty or more kilometers in a day. During the week, he continued working in Austria. They came and went like strangers in a train station. In April, she forgot his birthday – a bitter pill for him to swallow. He ended up opening a bottle of champagne with Lana. When Suzy finally came home, they were already in bed. The following day, he invited his family to dine in a fine restaurant, but Suzy excused herself. Oblivious of the occasion, she complained about having nothing to wear. She had gained more weight and was wearing the same pair of baggy trousers every day.

All the alarm bells were there, but he was so focused on sulking over his forgotten birthday.

Childish and egoistic.

He blamed himself to the point of losing his mind.

However, he blamed Victoria more. That controlling bitch had never allowed her daughter to breathe. She compensated for her lowly status as a pathetic elementary school history teacher by pushing Suzy to excel. Piano lessons, French courses, ballet, gym, healthy food, the perfect body to go with the perfect hair and makeup, the latest fashion. Her daughter's terrible mistake was falling in love with him, a young engineer from an average family. When Victoria dug deeper into his roots, she found out his grandfather was a prisoner of the communist regime, serving time on Goli Otok, Tito's gulag. Certainly no match for the daughter of Anton Jug, a high party official who accumulated wealth working for big state companies that drained their laborers in favor of a privileged life for the socialist nomenklatura. They hadn't welcomed him into the family. He was simply not good enough for Suzy, a gorgeous twenty-six year old with a brilliant future, who had just passed the bar exam, summa cum laude – the best result in the history of Slovenian law.

Henry would never forget the day he first met Suzy. His boss had sent him to fetch some paperwork from the largest law firm in Slovenia. Shyly, he had rung the bell. The clerk knew nothing about the documents, then Suzy entered the reception area.

"I'm Susanna Jug, one of the lawyers here."

"Henry Novak, engineer at Road Constructions Company."

"Hold on. I think I know what you're looking for."

She disappeared into the offices down the corridor leaving a lily-of-the-valley scent behind. He sat down while the clerk – a tall middle-aged man – winked at him. How could he know who she was and how every man at the firm called her the "Ice Princess"?

"These must be the papers you need." She sat next to him and opened the folder.

The sweet evocative scent wasn't only her perfume. It was her skin, slightly damp from the warm spring day.

He blushed and stuttered, "Thank you."

"Your boss has to sign here and here." She pointed at the lines at the bottom of the pages. "We need to have the contracts back by today in order to meet the public tender deadline. Can you bring everything back to us within an hour?"

He would have done anything for her – climb the moon, catch some stars.

"Yes," he managed to answer, wondering if she would still be there when he returned.

His boss was away, probably on a date with his mistress, so he had to wait until three to get him to sign the papers. Then, he ran back to the law firm. Only the clerk and Suzy were still there. She told him to wait in the lobby while she completed the paperwork.

She soon returned and handed the folders to the clerk. "Mr. Span, please take these to the court now. They're open until five today."

When the clerk was gone, she invited him to the conference room and offered him coffee and biscuits.

"What took you so long?"

He shrugged. "My boss was with a client."

"We know about his lunch-time clients. Remind him not to include hotel bills in his statements." She smiled.

They chatted until the clerk returned, then left the office together. They walked around Tivoli Park until dark. Later, he invited her for dinner. They kissed. It was the summer of 1990, a year before the independence. In July, they took his Citroen 2CV for a trip on the Dalmatian coast. He met Victoria on the way back when he brought Suzy to their summer beach house. She was waiting for them on the doorstep, her face the image of Leda – livid and angry. A communist snob. She couldn't believe her daughter had slept in a tent under the stars.

"Oh, we didn't sleep much, Mrs. Jug." He laughed happily.

The die was cast. She did not invite him in and had hated him ever since. It was a miracle that, on the contrary, Suzy seemed to love him more every day. They got married that same year on a sunny September day. He thought Suzy had gotten over her mother's ambitions and pressure. He loved her and they were happy. Victoria could never come between them.

Yet, on many occasions during their marriage, he caught his mother-in-law scheming against him. Pressuring Suzy to divorce him even after Lana was born. A conniving, controlling bitch of a mother. No wonder Suzy went out of her mind given the way Mother had treated her her whole life.

Victoria was six feet under and yet they still couldn't find peace with each other.

Anyway, he should have seen the signs.

He should have been there for her.

Instead, he had felt hurt at not being the center of his wife's attention.

So she forgot his birthday – so what?

Men were sorry creatures.

So were children.

Selfish creatures when a mother needed them.

In spite of her busy days at the university, Lana was upset and felt guilty, too. With Suzy in the hospital, they were both overwhelmed by new tasks.

Henry had to reorganize his work in Austria. He hired an on-site assistant and managed the building from Ljubljana. He drove there once a week to check on the situation and progress. Additionally, he looked in on matters in Suzy's office. Her secretary was a treasure. She knew everything and everybody, so they were able to put things on hold until she got back.

Now, he sat waiting in the park. He looked at the windows on the second floor where she was staying. She didn't want him to come in and fetch her; she wanted to go out to the park herself. Her psychiatrist requested him not to question her on what had triggered the breakdown as it wasn't his job. As a husband, he should just be there for her, try to listen and help her change the pattern that had brought her to her current state. When he suggested a holiday, the doctor advised against it. The last thing Suzy needed was travel stress. She needed peace, nature, kindness, love.

How did she feel about him?

Would they ever be able to rebuild their relationship?

Here she came. Pale face, hair in a ponytail, some makeup. A navy blue dress that hugged her hips, showing off the fullness of her body. A bag in her right. Ready to leave the walls of the hospital where she faced her worst fears. He stood up and gave her the roses.

"They're wonderful, Henry," she whispered with tears in her eyes.

"I love you, Suzy." He kissed her on the lips. "Everything is going to be okay."

Not expecting the kiss, she drew back. Her gaze was empty of emotions. She must have been filled with drugs. She turned to the sky and saw the horse-chestnut flowers. A soft breeze shook off the petals and tossed them playfully around.

She pointed in the air. "Look, Henry! It's snowing spring!"

He followed her gaze, troubled by what she meant. Then he understood. It was her greeting to life.

"Yes, darling," he said, putting an arm around her.

"Henry, I feel changed. For a long time, I had the feeling that crows were following me from the shadows. Black and evil, just waiting for the moment to seize my sanity. It was terrifying. I was afraid I would lose you and Lana."

"We were the ones who should have chased the crows away and protected you. We failed you, darling," he replied, caressing her cheek.

"No, I failed myself. I failed because I couldn't accept that I'm a flawed woman who makes mistakes. I was chasing the light in the mirror. I was filling in the image of Mother's ghosts. The doctor brought me back to earth. It's just me now."

He caressed her cheek with a palm of his hand.

"You are the best thing that has ever happened to me. I will never leave you, my love, never."

She put her arms around him and they stayed embraced under the snow of petals falling on their shoulders.

"Let's go home. Lana is waiting. She's got a surprise for you."

The mention of their daughter's name brought color to Suzy's cheeks. "Oh, what kind of surprise?"

Henry shook his head.

"I don't know, to be honest. She was very secretive about it," he replied, worried it was something that might cause stress to Suzy's fragile state of mind.

"Let's go home and see then."

She walked towards the parking lot.

Her first steps into a new life without Mother.
Without Mother telling her where to go and what to do.
There was only the three of them now: man, wife, and child forever.

Epilogue

> Counting the beats,
> Counting the slow heart beats,
> The bleeding to death of time in slow heart beats,
> Wakeful they lie.
>
> – Robert Graves, Counting the Beats

After the most expensive cup of coffee in Europe at St. Mark's Square, Vera and Suzy enjoyed walking along the canals and studying the rich architecture of Venice. Scarred and scary gargoyles on the façades of churches, lions on the pillars of the bridges, leaves and flowers etched in stone blooming for eternity. The air was crisp and the weather cold, the tourists' occupation in all facets and colors gone for the season. What a wonderful gift – a weekend for two at a luxury hotel in Venice.

At times, they walked hand in hand like lovers, the flow of their emotions too strong to hold back. No one gave them strange looks. Venice was, after all, the city of love – any love, straight or gay. Love and passion married to reason and entrepreneurship built this city centuries ago, and every summer the doge still threw a ring into the sea as a sign of Venice's allegiance to the sea.

Vera's phone beeped.

"Look, Sarah sent a footage of little Adam eating spinach." Vera proudly showed Suzy the screen.

"Oh, he's not eating it. He's spitting it out. No baby likes spinach!"

"Yeah, mashed potatoes, ice cream, bread – anything but fruits and vegetables. Sarah worries too much. She should relax. He gets enough vitamins."

Suzy smiled. Age floated wisdom and polished reason like sea-flushed driftwood on the beach. She could still remember her first years as a mother, though.

"Weren't we the same, Vera? I spent hours in the kitchen making vegetable puree and porridge. I even mixed yogurt with minced kiwi...Oh, those were the years."

Vera sighed. "You were a very apprehensive mother, Suzy. Maybe I wasn't attentive enough, though."

Suzy stopped and put her arms around Vera's shoulder. "Will you stop blaming yourself? He died and there was nothing you could have done."

Vera's eyes filled with tears. "I never told you why I blame myself for Luca's death. Maybe it's time I do."

They sat down for lunch in a restaurant with a large window on the Grand Canal. There was time for words and time for silence. By the end of Vera's account, Suzy's heart broke.

"You were two shipwrecked children, you and Adam. You only had each other to love."

Vera looked at the waves on the Grand Canal glowing orange and purple in the early sunset. She missed Adam every day of her life. Sometimes, when she walked alone in the woods, she would talk to him in a low voice. She would tell him about Gregory and Lucia, their beautiful wedding at Bled, Lucia's honest and kind Argentinian parents who had moved to Slovenia, his second grandchild on the way. About the company and how competently Gregory was managing the business, about Sarah's last year of studies, about herself going back to publishing after a few months of helping out at the company.

What she couldn't tell him, he would read in the memoir she was writing since summer: My Life with Adam. Everything would be in the book: from the little boy abandoned at Trieste's

Ponte Rosso Square to the owner of a business empire that was built with passion and hard work. A loving husband. A dedicated father. Everything.

Tears often interrupted her writing. Memories, regrets, sensations long gone. The words brought up all the suppressed emotions, all the hopes and fears that invaded her heart. Writing was the bleeding to death of time in slow heart beats. Still, it was a sort of catharsis, too. She felt relieved and lightened, like now, after finally telling another living soul about the baby she had killed in her womb as a teenager.

"They say you shouldn't speak ill of the dead, but your mother was a bitch like mine, Vera."

"I guess they were both children of war. That's how survivors are."

Suzy shook her head. "When I found the letter she had written for posterity, it was so full of shit I found it hard to stomach."

Vera nodded. "I know. How could she judge you after death? After all you've done for her…"

"She could because she didn't love me. The look she gave me on the day before she died. Green pupils like two drops of Murano glass, transfixed, as though she had seen the world beyond, yet vibrating to convey a message. Before I got hold of that damned letter, I thought it was merely a reproach to the living. I must die while you go on living, you know. The usual bitterness and regrets. I could empathize. Mother clung to life like a tick to skin. She wouldn't let go and was ready to endure any pain for one second more. I kind of admired her fighting spirit."

Vera stretched her hand over the table. "I'll never understand how anyone could not love their only daughter, the angel of their old age. You were much too kind, Suzy. She did not deserve it."

Suzy sipped the red wine, wondering if she could ever deal with the hurt. Maybe time would heal the wound. However, she could never forget the words.

Dear Susanna,

You're reading this letter because I'm dead. I trust the funeral was as I have wished. I love you more than you can think. You will understand one day that a mother's love is the only true love. Men come and go, children egoistically seek their luck, yet mothers love forever.

Do not grieve for me too long. Rather get your life and office in order. Your husband is a good-for-nothing. In spite of his kindness to me during these last months, he neither deserves nor loves you. I didn't want to spoil our last moments together, but it's time you face reality: He's having an affair. You know my sources never fail. I am sorry. If you make more time for yourself and get in shape, you can be a very attractive woman. Being a terrific lawyer and a loving mother, I am sure you can find a better match.

My will is deposited with the public notary Kern at Slovenska Street 12 in Ljubljana. Please don't be disappointed. Lana, your daughter and my granddaughter, is my only heir. Because of your relationship with Henry, I cannot trust you with the estates and monies your father and I have accumulated through hard work over the years.

I hope you will understand this.

Have a good life and think of me sometimes,

Your loving Mommy

The hatred Mother spilled was like poison running slowly through Suzy's veins. The intention to destroy her marriage and damage her life. Where did she get such venom? Her sources never failed. Suzy had not confronted her husband, neither had she shown him the letter. She did show it to her psychiatrist, who explained why a child cannot thrive in the shadow of such a mother. It helped Suzy enormously. The readings, her mother's sickness of mind, her manipulative nature as a result of an unhappy childhood. She was trying to understand and forgive Mother, find mercy for her deep in her heart.

She didn't care for Mother's fortune nor was she hurt by her distrust.

"You're a brilliant lawyer, but I cannot trust you with the inheritance because you love a husband who's shagging another." Fine. If only I'd known what you thought of me while you were alive, Mother.

What pushed Suzy over the edge was the unrequited love of a little girl.

She broke down and cried. "Well, I don't regret it. I mean, all the care and love I gave her. I did it for me. I want to look myself in the mirror when I put on my makeup in the morning and see a person, not an ass."

"She's responsible for your breakdown, Suzy."

"Henry and Lana picked up the shards and glued them together. And my new psychiatrist is so cute. I have so much fun with him."

Vera looked at her uncertainly. "Who do you mean?"

"Vic, my golden retriever!"

They burst into laughter.

"Cheers to psychiatric dogs! Maybe I should get one, too."

"It's the best therapy ever. A long walk twice a day. He always wants to play, stays faithfully at my feet, and follows me around the house like a satellite. I love him. He's a king. He's charmed even Laika. That bitch jumps like a puppy with him."

"Well, a Latino lover with a six pack couldn't do a better job. You've lost weight and look gorgeous, my friend."

They left the restaurant and headed for their hotel where they would spend the evening at the spa. Sauna and massage.

The twilight obscured the narrow streets of Venice, but the women did not care for the long shadows dragging around the corners. They were ghosts from the past and their place was not in this world.

Tomorrow the sun will rise and shine over Venice and chase death away.

One day, though, death will come to exact its toll on them. Memento mori.
Until then, there were heart beats to count.
Tick-tock, tick-tock, tick-tock.

THE END

Printed in Poland
by Amazon Fulfillment
Poland Sp. z o.o., Wrocław